I0554234

The Indian Prince

www.barbarianspy.com

WARNING: This book is for sale to **ADULT AUDIENCES ONLY**. Contains graphic bisexual and gay male sex, anal sex, non-graphic violence, and menage sex all of which may be considered offensive by some readers.

All sexually active characters in this work are at least 18 years of age.

This book is copyright © habu 2017
habu asserts his right to be known as the author of this work.
Published by BarbarianSpy in 2017
Cover design © S Bush 2017
Cover images:all manipulated; head© Francesco Cura | Dreamstime.com Indian palace © Socrates | Dreamstime.com
ISBN Paperback: 978-1-925568-17-2
All rights reserved

No part of this book may be reproduced in any form, except for the inclusion of brief quotations in a review or article, without written permission from the author or publisher.

All characters in this book are the product of the author's imagination and no resemblance to real people, or implication of events occurring in actual places, is intended.

BarbarianSpy
Toronto, Australia

The Indian

Prince

Habu

TABLE OF CONTENTS

Chapter One

"The Rawal wishes to know if you play tennis."

"Certainly," I answered. And, of course, I did. The angle had all been researched.

"Perhaps a game at 4:00 PM on Tuesday on the palace courts, then?"

"Yes, yes, of course, I would be honored." And, of course, I would be. I turned to where I could see Roger Allard, the U.S. chief of station in the remote suzerainty of Sravasti, and saw him give me a smile and a thumbs up.

I turned back to the Kshatriyas, the term in Sravasti for the crown prince's—or, as known here, the Rawal's—chief adviser. "The Rawalina is a beautiful woman. But her skin is so fair; I'm surprised she came this morning. This

7

must really be boring for her." I almost choked off the last few words, as Roger's thumb had gone down and he was giving me a little frown.

"That is not the Rawalina," the Kshatriyas said. "That is the prince's mistress, not his wife. You are correct that the Rawalina would not appear here today."

The prince's chief adviser, Mir Yusaf Adil, spoke in a firm tone, but I didn't notice any tensing up or disapproval in his voice. Indeed, he was still smiling, and he had a firm grip on my elbow that didn't waver. I could say the same for the stiff, taller, and bulkier graybeard who was standing beside him. That was the king's adviser, General Ambedkar Sungar, who Allard had warned me to avoid but not to cross. He was being checked out, upon intelligence received, for possible ties to Al-Qaeda.

We were on the tarmac of the hidden airstrip in the miniscule Indian domain of Balrampur, a strategic almost-autonomous ministate lodged under the belly of western Nepal. It was hot as blazons standing on the asphalt under the summer Indian sun, which was why I was surprised the Rawal—the prince—had brought a woman to this exercise. She was all decked out in a red silk sari, head scarf and all, that was only marred by the large-lens sunglasses almost obliterating her face. Still, she looked like the nearest thing

8

to a cool cucumber of any of us out here, if more than a little bit bored.

The bored part I could easily understand. We had brought the prince out here for a look-see at the Fairchild Magnus photoreconnaissance plane we'd just received in the inventory. We thought a ten-minute inspection and that would be that, but we were being dumb there and should have known better. The prince had gone over the aircraft more carefully and in more detail than even our persnickety ground crew had done when it arrived. We'd all been standing out here in the sweltering heat, in formation, for the better part of an hour.

I was here because I'd flown the Magnus in. I did fly photorecon now and again still, but that wasn't the reason I had flown the Magnus in to our secret airbase in Balrampur.

But we should have known better about the interest the prince would show in the aircraft. The Rawal of Balrampur, Bhadur Khan, had been a problem since his early teens. He had been rebellious and stubborn and never bright about anything but mechanics. He lived and breathed military and airplanes. As the future Badshah of Shwetambar, the virtual king of the satrapy of Balrampur, however, he was both a potential thorn in the side and a future ruler to contend with for both the people of

Balrampur and, as misfortune would have it, the United States.

With U.S. help, the unruly Rawal was kept under somewhat reasonable control by feeding his passion for military equipment, especially airplanes. Not yet twenty-five, he had been a student at nearly every military academy that the Western powers could put him through, including Sandhurst in England and even, as a special student, the U.S. Air Force Academy in Colorado Springs. He actually had a talent for piloting planes, and his various handlers kept him focused and only an occasional danger to others by steeping him in military gadgetry.

The Fairchild Magnus photoreconnaissance plane was just such a new gadget. And, conveniently—or, more precisely, as a major foreign policy headache—a major secret U.S. photoreconnaissance base, from which surveillance was conducted over Pakistan and Afghanistan in the east, Tibet to the north and, at one time, Vietnam, Cambodia, and Laos to the southeast, was hosted in Balrampur by the Badshah of Shwetambar.

Most who look at modern-day India see a unified country that rose out of a collection of princedoms in which various maharajas of various titles ruled as if feudal kings. This is a surface understanding, though. To a large extent and in all practical purposes, many of the fiefdoms continue to exist—with their traditional ruling families reigning more or less as they had always done down from the Mughal era.

Balrampur, a small but strategically placed satrapy, thus was of paramount importance to the United States—and, indeed, to the allies of the United States. Its ruler, the Badshah of Shwetambar had always been a steadfast friend of the United States. But he had not really been seen or heard from beyond his inner court for several months. Anyone who tried to get to the Badshah ran squarely against a stonewalling General Sungar, who exercised the privilege of taking the matter to the Badshah and returning with his answer. Increasingly, the Badshah's son, the Rawal, who was rumored also to be under the sway of Sungar, was becoming the focus of concern and hope.

And the Rawal had eclectic personal tastes.

"Is there something I should know or bring when I come to tennis on Tuesday?" I asked of the Kshatriyas, Mir Yusaf Adil. Since Sungar was standing close, I didn't try to whisper below his hearing—but Adil was the prince's man, so I was within propriety to be querying him on the matter.

"Only that you lose at tennis—and at anything else the Rawal desires of you," Adil answered, a sparkle in his eye. "Do you understand?"

"Yes," I answered. And indeed I did. Roger Allard had let me know in no uncertain terms what I would be expected to be prepared to do on this special assignment I had drawn. As I noted, I hadn't just been needed to fly the Magnus in. I was also here because I was an agent of the CIA's Candy Store unit.

I took another look at Adil. He was older than I was, but certainly not yet forty. He was so darkly handsome, slender, and sensuously graceful that I rather regretted that my assignment was the Rawal rather than his Kshatriyas. The Rawal was quite presentable in his own right. His dedication to exercise and developing his body was only second to his passion for aeronautics. And he was taller and more solid of body than most of his subjects were. His mother had been of high-caste, mixed Persian and Indian origin, which had squared his jaw and given the Rawal an almost Western look, although his skin was as dusky as others from this region of India. Adil could have been a Bollywood hunk star. The Rawal unmistakably was a solid, rugged military leader type.

It's just that the Rawal—the prince—wasn't all that bright, and he had a dogged look about him that was half pout and half warning that he could explode in an act of craziness at the least provocation.

The way the Rawal had looked at me as we were together in the cockpit of the Magnus and I was showing him how the controls worked assured me that he was interested. It was my assignment to make him interested. But it also sent a chill up my spine. I got the distinct impression that his interest was completely self-centered, with a streak of cruelty—that there may be a way I could serve him, but that there would be no reward or consideration for me in it.

But this was the job. This was what my specialized section of the Agency was designed for—to serve the baser instincts of men and women alike to suborn their cooperation.

When I had been called into Sam Winterberry's office in Langley and he'd told me I was flying a Fairchild Magnus, a follow-on from the Fairchild Merlin photorecon plane, into Sravasti, India, my initial responses were "Where the fuck is that? I've never heard of such a place" and "I'm no longer in the photorecon business. What's the angle?"

"I'm glad you haven't heard of Sravasti, Craig. Our operation there is one of our best-kept secrets and we like it to stay that way. It's the capital of a small Indian state called Balrampur, near the Nepal border. We have a consulate there. But what the consulate really is fully composed of is a CIA station."

"A consulate? Or even a station. Why would we need either there?"

"For the same reason we need you to fly one of the new Fairchild Magnuses there. We have a secret home strip there for photoreconnaissance over several high-profile target areas there. So we take a great interest in Balrampur."

"But why me? Doesn't the Agency have any other jet jockey available to go there? I haven't even checked out on the Magnus. That has come in since my time in that field."

"For us to stay in Balrampur, we must keep the local potentate in our pocket. In this case, the local potentate is the Badshah of Shwetambar, and as far as we know, he might be dead. His people—meaning one person, really, his closest adviser—haven't let us at him for months, and he's old and feeble—and there has been a rumor of a bad heart for some years. We even have intell claiming his wife is slowly poisoning him. She's from a rival family for

14

ascendance in Balrampur. She forced her son, the Rawal, to marry her niece last year—which led to the Rawal ending all communication with his mother."

"And you want me to revive him—this Badshah?" I had meant it as a joke, but there wasn't much humor in Sam Winterberry and I certainly hadn't drawn any out of him now.

"Well, this does bring us to the reason why we are sending you in with the Magnus. You are the only one cross trained in what we need there at this moment."

"Ah, who needs to be fucked then?" I asked. If we weren't going to have a mirth fest, I thought we might as well get down to brass tacks.

"The Badshah's son is a man of wide tastes. He's also been very hard to handle. He may stand in our path, though, as soon as there is a change of rulers in Balrampur. He needs to be handled. And so do any of the advisers around the Badshah and Rawal, as necessary. The primary ones all have the taste for it, we understand—in the dominant position."

"Ah," I had said. And that was my assignment.

It wasn't until I got to Sravasti and was sitting in the consulate cum Agency station with Roger Allard, the chief of station, that I learned how delicate the mission was.

15

"He what?" I asked, taken by surprise.

"He shot and killed his wife's secretary last month. He is unpredictable and volatile. He was rebelling against having been forced to marry his cousin."

"I've heard that the marriage was arranged by his mother to further her own family's interests. But why shoot the secretary?"

"He either got in the way or he was doing something the Rawal didn't want him to do."

"Ah, a male secretary. Fucking the Rawalina perhaps? A jealous rage?"

"We doubt it. The marriage was arranged entirely by the Badshahrina and, we understand, was barely consummated. As far as we can determine, the Rawal never has been impressed by his wife, which is probably a gross understatement of his hatred for the whole idea of being married to her. We doubt he cared whether the secretary was fucking her. The most likely situation—and the one feeding the rumor mills throughout Balrampur—was that the Rawal was aiming for his wife and the secretary just got in the way."

"Ouch. So, somewhat of a nut job then."

"I wouldn't say that outside of this office. They take lese majeste very, very seriously here. It's the same as high

16

treason would be in America. We need to keep him calm, concentrated on the pursuits that interest him, and on our side. We've run out of foreign schools to send him to. The palace wanted him back home—probably because his father's demise is imminent, if it's not already passed us by—and we have to think up new ways to contain and control him here."

"And that's where I come in?"

"Yes. If we can we want to get you as close to him as possible. And as important to him as possible."

"You don't perceive this as a short-term assignment, do you?"

"Not if we're successful."

"And here I wasn't told to come with more than one suitcase."

"If we're successful, you won't be needing much in the way of clothing."

"When and where do we start?"

"In less than an hour and out there on the tarmac, where you parked the Magnus. The Rawal is coming today to inspect it—and, we hope, to inspect you as well."

"Nothing like jumping right into an assignment," I said. I was sitting and looking at a photograph of the Rawal. I briefly contemplated whether I'd mind being fucked by him. I'd taken on uglier—and certainly older and less fit—assignments before. But I couldn't tell. There were aspects of him that were attractive, but even in the photograph I could see the edge of cruelty and insanity. Perhaps if his was the only visage in the photograph I would have found him quite acceptable. But it wasn't. Standing behind him was a far more alluring man, older than the Rawal but much more darkly handsome and arousing. His presence in the photograph made it difficult for me to concentrate on the Rawal.

I learned within the hour that the other man was the Rawal's chief adviser, The Kshatriyas, Mir Yusaf Adil.

Chapter Two

Mir Yusaf Adil met my limousine when it pulled up to what they said was the Sports House within the complex of pools and various game courts, in addition to stables and a polo ring, that was in fairly distant sight of the palace itself. The palace complex seemed to be huge—almost taking up, it appeared, half the territory of all of Balrampur.

"Come on through here, Mr. Townsend. I'll show you where the changing room is. And shorts only, please."

"Shorts only? Sun's pretty strong today."

"The Rawal sets the scenes around here. He's out there already without a shirt."

So, I just didn't shirt up in the locker room, but I did lay on the suntan lotion. It was fine with me. I was

19

supposed to seduce this prince—and I didn't have anything to be ashamed of it he wanted to ogle my naked torso. It would enable me to cut closer to the chase in this assignment I had.

It turns out that the prince had a pretty impressive torso of his own, and it didn't hurt me in terms of getting in a mood to watch him playing. His mistress, who I had learned was a Bollywood actress going by the single name Aruna, sat beside the court at a table under an umbrella that the prince and I retreated to after the odd-numbered games. The rest of the retinue in attendance had to stand at attention in the sun in a semicircle around the table and play statue the entire match. Only Adil and General Sungar had the privilege of standing in the shadow of the umbrella—but they too played statue unless there was something the prince wanted from them.

Aruna sat there in a sky blue sari and those big-lens sunglasses, jangled her gold bangle bracelets on both wrists and ankles, and sipped on whatever pink-colored drink they kept exchanging for a new one before she hit bottom while taking little drags on a cigarette in a gold-plated holder. She looked extremely bored and not at all "there." As far as looks, though, she was quite "there."

I was halfway through the match—that was hard fought, but with the prince "miraculously" winning every strategic point—before I realized that Aruna was subtly changing her position. She was slouching farther back in her chair, with her hips forward in the seat, and the folds of her sari were progressively separating and inching off her long, long legs. Well into the second set, she was widening her legs. Her pubes were shaved in a precise triangle.

I didn't know whether Aruna was flashing for the prince or for me. I certainly hoped that the prince either assumed it was for him—I was quickly learning that he assumed everything was for him—or that he didn't mind sharing the sights.

At the end of the match, the prince just stalked over to Aruna, snapped his fingers, and the two of them, with the whole entourage in tow except for the Kshatriyas, Mir Yusaf Adil, walked off toward the Sports House. No "thank you for the match," or "you played well," or "get out of my sight" from Bhadur Khan, the Rawal, which I thought was a bit brusque of him. He did win, and I did make him look good doing it, so I couldn't see that he had a beef about anything—except maybe Aruna's exhibitionism. But that was her, not me. I didn't have my tongue hanging out or anything. Aruna didn't even glance my way, so I guess her show was for him.

"Do you ride?"

I looked around at Adil. For a brief moment I wondered if he was asking if I topped, and I wondered what was the magic answer that would set well with the prince. But then the Rawal's adviser brought focus to the question.

"The horses? Do you ride; play polo? I thought you might like to take a look at the stables and at the horses before you go back to the Sports House and shower. You did quite well at tennis, thank you. I could see that you were doing what needed to be done—and that perhaps you didn't need to."

"I have ridden horses, yes," I answered. "But usually only when there is no other form of transportation available. I normally like to fly."

"The Rawal likes to fly too. Perhaps you are thinking that flying is his sole interest in you?"

"I think I have been well briefed," I answered. At that point I wasn't sure that the prince had any interest in me at all. He didn't speak to me at all during changeovers, and I didn't get the looks of interests from him that usually clued me that a man was interested. He had been quite rigid and brusque with me, actually. But I did need to establish with Adil that I was available.

"So, you will know what is expected? And you remember that the prince must have his way in all matters? I do what I can for the interests of your country here. I don't think either your country or I would want there to be any misunderstandings."

"No misunderstandings. But I don't think I particularly impressed the prince."

"Don't let his manner deceive you. And when I asked about whether you rode, did you perhaps get the wrong first impression?"

"Yes, perhaps. But the answer is that I don't usually ride, but if that's what is called for—"

"Very good; that won't be a problem here. Part of the tension in our closed society is that most of the men of the court like to do the riding."

I gave him a glance, and he was smiling wryly. I certainly hoped that was the case with him as well.

"Come," he continued, "let us take in the stables. As you can imagine, we are quite proud of our thoroughbreds. And polo?"

"I haven't even watched. I'm afraid I know nothing about the game—other than that it requires a lot of skill."

"But if the Rawal wanted you to play?"

"I would play. And he, naturally, would win. If he asked me to ride, I'd ride. If he wanted to ride, I'd be ridden."

"Except, of course, the Rawal never asks. He demands. He also, I must add, never plays. Nothing is just play for him." That stung a bit, but Adil just smiled and led me toward the stables. I was actually grateful. He was educating me, which probably was the whole purpose of this little walk alone with him. And he was doing it as subtly and sensitively as I could expect.

When we came back, he guided me into the locker room again and handed me a towel—and then stood there and watched me as I showered. At first I had to turn away from him as best I could, because I found him highly desirable—and he'd be able to see that in his effect on my body. I had melted to his touch on my bare shoulders as he guided me around the stable area.

"No, please, Mr. Townsend. Do not turn from me. It is my duty to report to the Rawal what is on offer."

"Very well," I answered, and I turned full frontal to him, still embarrassed that I was hard—and getting harder under his scrutiny. If it had any effect on him, though, he didn't betray it.

"Thank you. Turn please and bend over."

I did so, and almost immediately he was behind me, with the palms of his hands on my buttocks.

"Hold them parted, please."

As I complied, I heard the snap of the latex glove, and thus I wasn't surprised—responding to the invasion with only a grunt—when I felt first one, and then a second, cold, gloved finger pushing into my channel. I felt his hand squeeze one of my butt cheeks when he had finished his examination, which I marked as the only sign from him that wasn't clinical. I felt the disappointment that he hadn't moved to invade me with more than his gloved fingers.

"Thank you. You may dry off and dress now."

The voice came from across the shower room, at the locker room door. When I stood and turned, he was gone.

When I came out and dried, he handed me a diaphanous white caftan he called a sherwani, telling me that was all that I needed, and then we padded down a corridor to a set of large, ornate-wood double doors, guarded by two burly guards in the elaborate Balrampur military livery. The two guards opened the door and, nudging me forward, Adil disappeared.

I was standing in a large, ornately furnished room, with so much vibrant color everywhere that I had difficulty focusing. The walls appeared to be white marble, as was as much of the flooring as I could see around the edges of Oriental carpets. Fabric pillows were strewn everywhere—in different, brilliant colors, probably all silk—and a king-sized platform bed between marble pillars draped with red silk stood in the middle of the room.

General Ambedkar Sungar was standing in the shadows, stiff and arms crossed, looking every bit like a stuffed eunuch in the background of an Arabian nights film. His face was set in what I was beginning to think was a permanent scowl.

The prince and Aruna were on the bed, in the altogether other than Aruna's bangle bracelets on her wrists and ankles and a gauzy scarf around her torso that wasn't so thick that I couldn't make out one rouged nipple set in a pendulous breast or Prince Bhadur Khan's ringed hand covering the other under the scarf.

Aruna wasn't wearing her huge sunglasses now. She was wearing a smile and she was looking at me with that smile as I stood just inside the doorway—the doors of which were shut in simultaneous motions by the two guards. I could see the outline of the front of the prince's body, because he was larger and darker than the actress, but she was lying stretched out on his body, both of which were propped up by a sea of pillows. Both were facing me.

The prince tipped Aruna's body up to show that his cock was buried in her ass. The lips of her other opening were rouged and both that and her mouth seemed to be pouting at me. She had a nicely rounded belly, with what appeared to be a ruby in her navel. My first instinct was to want to fish that out with my tongue, which I bet was exactly her thought in having put it there.

"Join me. Inside her," That's all the prince said, and it didn't sound like a request.

I pulled the sherwani over my head, and stood there for a moment as I dropped it at my feet. Aruna laughed a low, throaty laugh, and I saw her lick her lips.

Although this was unexpected, I was ready for it. I'd been on the rise since Adil watched me shower, and the view of the prince, who at least from what I could see of the base of his cock was well hung, fucking the gorgeous, almost alabaster-skinned actress in the ass, brought me to full staff.

Something about the way the Rawal had given his command made me decide I wouldn't want him to have to repeat it, so I strode over to the bed and climbed up onto it on my knees and crawled over their bodies. I leaned down and tongued around Aruna's navel to let her know I could have claimed the ruby with my teeth if I'd wanted to, and her rounded little belly shook like a bowl of Jell-O. I then lifted my head and took her lips in mine, while I fisted my cock to between her rouged nether lips. I found her clit with it and rubbed the tip of my staff up and down there until I felt her shudder and her lips—both above and below—open wider to me and she took my tongue lightly between her teeth.

I allowed the head of my cock to lower to between her labia and press there ever so slightly until Aruna moaned in anticipation of the long, deep slide, and then I dragged it back to rub against her clit, eliciting the same moan. Dragging back down, poising, and then the long sheathing as she shuddered and groaned.

I could feel him as I entered her, churning in her other channel, and I worked to adjust my rhythm to his as I ran my hands up her sides and under the scarf. I buried my face between her breasts and I could feel the prince squeezing them. Aruna twitched as he gripped her nipples between thumb and forefinger. He tugged at my hair and moved my face up and over her breast and I sucked on her nipple.

"Both. The ass," he hissed. And I accommodated him, pulling my hips back, as her body trembled form the loss of me, and then moving my cock to Aruna's ass with my hand, finding the base of the prince's cock still there, and slowly working my cock in over his. It was truly cock rubbing on cock inside her now. That lasted only a few moments. I felt Aruna shaking uncontrollably, and I knew she was trying to suppress groans, but wasn't completely able to do so.

I felt him pull out of her ass and then move from underneath her. He was gone from us, and I moved my cock from her ass back to her cunt. She murmured her thanks. I felt the prince's hands on my hips, so I was prepared for what was coming. But still I gasped and arched my back as he moved inside of me.

I fucked Aruna in the cunt and Bhadur Khan fucked me in the ass for several minutes. The prince said nothing for that time. He just grunted and groaned and did what he could do to reach for my tonsils from the inside. Aruna was moaning in measured waves that matched my rhythm— which matched the prince's rhythm. Women weren't my favorite, but I knew what to do, and she seemed to be enjoying it. I wasn't minding the back channel work myself. He was both long and thick—and in good shape.

"Aruna. Leave."

I pulled out to help Aruna squirm out from underneath me.

When we were alone, the prince pulled out of me and signaled with the movement of his hands that I was to turn on my back, which I did. He was standing between my legs, and I reached up with my hands and cupped his pecs—which obviously wasn't what he wanted, because he backhanded me hard across the cheek, with the ruby in the big ring on his finger slashing a line of blood under my cheekbone.

I laid back then, leaving it for him to show me what he wanted. What he wanted was to piston me deep and thump on my chest and abs with his fists and twist my nipples until he brought tears to my eyes.

My second mistake was to suggest he might want to lighten up, which only upped the action. His cock was big enough, but he moved a hand down there as well, and slid fingers in around his cock and stretched my channel to where I was afraid I'd be split. If he'd wanted to double me with one of the guards at the door, it could have been done. And having been with him inside Aruna, I wouldn't have been surprised if that was where we were going. I needed to make him explode and simmer down.

So, I went in the other direction, pumping him back hard with my hips and rotating my channel on his cock and being very vocal. This eventually made him come inside me with a huff on each of three final plunges.

Then he just backed up, turned around, and headed for the doors that I had entered. I gasped, I hoped not audibly, when I saw his back, buttocks, and the backs of his legs as he walked away. There were welts on them. Taking into account the demeanor he'd been showing me, I had visions of an ascetic monk, flagellating himself in a barren stone cell. This was one weird prince.

The double doors opened simultaneously as he approached them and then closed again in his wake. Just like on the tennis court. No smile or frown or a word to give me any clue at all what the sex had done for him. Just like that, he was gone.

I was alone in the dimly lit room then. But not really alone, I realized, as I sensed movement off in the shadows. The seemingly stuffed eunuch came to life. General Sungar moved over toward the bed. I froze when I saw the cruel leer on his face and the riding crop in his hand. Drumming in my brain was Allard's admonishment to avoid him, if possible, but to accommodate him, if necessary. There was no avoiding him here and under these circumstances, so, as he approached, I smiled up at him and widened my legs as he grabbed for one of my ankles.

His other hand went up into the folds of the draperies of one of the stone pillars at the bottom corner of the bed, and I tensed in recognition as he extracted and pulled down black nylon ankle restraints. I just laid there and watched as he trussed up, first one of my legs, and then the other to a restraint pulled down from the other pillar. I made the mistake of trying to raise my torso then, thinking to draw him down to me to show that I would obey whatever he asked of me, but he caught me on the chin with a slap of the riding crop and I fell back onto the bed as my head snapped back.

He didn't have to say a word. I knew what was coming—and that it was a test of whether I would just go with it.

He came around to one side of the bed and, resigned, I extended my arm to be restrained by a cuff brought up from the bed frame at the side. I hadn't quite prepared for his next move. I assumed he would fuck me then, just to show me the power he had in this palace. But he didn't do that right away. He stood between my legs and began to flick at my cock and balls with his riding crop. The more I writhed—more at the fear of what might be than what he was actually doing—the harder and faster he flicked. I tried to contain myself, tears forming in my closed eyes, but, not being able to help myself, I howled my pain and frustration. That was what he was waiting for. I heard him laugh, and then I opened my eyes and looked down my body to see him jack up his sherwani to reveal a hairy belly and pubes and a thickish, hard cock.

His thrust inside me was powerful, brutal, and all consuming. When he was fully saddled, and I could feel the tickle of his hairy balls against the tender skin of my inner thighs, he held. All of my senses went to the throbbing of his thick staff inside me, wondering, fearing, how brutally he would pump me.

When the fucking began, it was total, his bulb finding air, fully evacuating, and then slurping just inside to the rim of the glans, a gentle rotation, and then the long slide to full sheathing. This was followed by another total withdrawal. Me gasping at both points—the denial and the total possession.

He fucked me slowly, with little flicks on my chest, belly, cock and balls with his riding crop. His flow was long, drowning, delivered as deep inside me as he could reach. As cruel as he was, I wanted it to go on and on. I told him so—not just because I was mindful of my instructions to accommodate him, but also because I wanted him to take me again, there and then. He laughed a low, guttural laugh.

"I was going to take from you again, anyway," he growled.

And then he did.

Finally done, he simply released me from my bonds and turned and left the room via a small door at the back of the room. I moved my body up to where I was fully on the bed and laid there, moaning, and eventually dozed off.

When I was fully awake again, I waited there, wondering what was going to happen next. Nothing did. I seemed to have been forgotten. With a groan, I pulled myself off the bed and leaned down and scooped up the sherwani I'd come in with. I shrugged into it and walked toward the doors I had entered. Just as for the prince, they opened for me as if automatic. When I got to the other side, though, I saw that it was Indian automatic, where human power was cheaper and less complicated than anything technical.

I asked the guards who had opened the door which way was to anywhere I should be going, not knowing where I was going. But I thought that, if I got back to the locker room, I could dress in my street clothes and maybe, while I was doing that, give some thought on how to get back to the station and let Roger know that my usefulness was over. The prince obviously was a one-night stand type of guy and had taken what he wanted from me and had now lost interest—if he'd ever been interested in more than just getting his rocks off with someone new each time.

Of course neither of the guards responded to my questions. They undoubtedly had been told that I wasn't really even there—and they only kept their cushy jobs on either side of these doors because they did exactly what they were told.

I found that I knew my way back to the locker room, but I didn't make it there. As I was walking down the corridor, I heard a woman's voice—Aruna, I presumed—really going to town in angry Hindi. I'd started to learn the language, but there was no way I was keeping up with what she was jabbering about. When she screamed, I instinctively turned and opened and door to the room where I thought the scream was coming from.

It was some sort of reception room—handsomely appointed—with French doors leading out to a graveled motor court. Standing in front of me, his back to me, was Bhadur Khan, the prince. He was wearing an emerald green sherwani and a nasty-looking handgun.

At the other side of the room stood the woman, not jabbering now, her mouth covered with the back of her hand, and her bugged-out eyes plastered at the handgun, the barrel of which was pointed at her.

It wasn't Aruna. After my earlier faux pass on the secret airbase tarmac where I'd assumed she was the prince's Rawalina, Roger Allard made quite sure that I would know what Vimala, the Rawalina of Balrampur, looked like. She looked just like the woman on the other side of the room—even though the woman in the photograph looked regal and this one looked some crazy combination of frazzled, terrified, and angry.

The real problem was that Roger told me that he certainly hoped I never saw Bhadur Khan and his wife in the same room together, because the prince had said if he ever laid eyes on her again he'd shoot her. Visions of him already trying to and killing her secretary instead raced through my head—nonsensically with me as the secretary standing between the Rawalina and the line of that gun barrel.

Chapter Three

"Oh, there you are, Rawal. I was looking for you. I hope I'm not being too forward, but it occurred to me that you might want to fly the Fairchild Magnus, not just check it out. I think you've flown all of our new . . ."

I walked into the room and started speaking like I'd seen nothing of what was happening in there. I was flying on instinct here. I tried to keep my eyes level with the prince's as he slowly turned toward me. Every fiber of me wanted to look for where the barrel of the gun was pointed, but I knew I couldn't even acknowledge that there was a gun in the room. The prince's eyes were smoldering with anger as he turned, but that was replaced, almost instantly, with the look of a young boy in a video arcade.

Bingo. I'd guessed right on what would divert his attention.

"When?"

"We could start today . . . right now, if you wish. There will be preflight instruction and then you'll have to go up with a pilot . . . I could do all of that. Two days tops and we could have you flying the Magnus. You'd be among the first twenty pilots that have done so—certainly the first one who wasn't an American."

"We go now then." It was as if the slate had been wiped clean. The prince had forgotten all about his wife, cowering behind a sofa across the room now, and didn't even seem to be aware that he was holding a hand gun. He briskly departed the room and was barking orders for a car to be brought around as he strode away into and down the corridor.

I only then felt my adrenaline giving way, and I reached out for the back of a straight chair to keep myself from falling. I had other support, though. The Kshatriyas, Mir Yusaf Adil, was behind me, and he put an arm around me to keep me from collapsing. Two women and a man filtered around us and raced across the room to the Rawalina's side.

The Rawalina was gathering her strength again, and the anger returned to her face. "That woman. He has that . . . harlot . . . here, in the palace."

Are you talking to me? I wanted to toss at her. Not a glimmer of appreciation that the life I most likely saved was hers. If she were my wife maybe I'd want to shoot her too.

I could clearly understand her Hindi now; she was speaking in distinct, measured, angry tones.

"We will speak of this later, Rawalina," Adil spoke out—in English. "If you raise your voice, he may refocus and be back. You didn't tell me you would come today. You almost got yourself killed. I suggest you return immediately to your quarters in the palace. I will call the Badshahrina to meet you there. We must talk of this, the three of us. But go now—while you still can—directly out to the courtyard. I see you have a car there. I would suggest that you have your driver take you around to your apartments by the service road so that you don't cross paths with him again."

The Rawalina tossed her head in a defiance that she certainly hadn't been projecting when I first entered the room. But, brushing the clinging hands of her servants away, she turned, waited for her man to open a French door leading out to the motor court, and majestically sailed out of the building and into a limousine, the rear door popping open for her as she reached the vehicle.

Adil and I were alone then, although there was so much bustling about in the corridor, the reel of life in the palace now revolving double time following the moments when all held their breath anticipating the firing of the handgun. Adil still had a supporting arm around me. I didn't need the support anymore, but I wouldn't reject the opportunity to be close to him.

"You spoke to her in English," I said, rather nonsensically, I later thought when I replayed the scene to myself.

"I wanted you to hear and to understand. The little bitch nearly got herself killed. And it isn't like she didn't barely escape such a fate before. I wanted you to know how cataclysmic the event was that your fast thinking saved us all from."

"Does she have a separate palace?"

"No, she lives here—in a remote wing of the main palace."

"And she needs a car to get there from here?"

"It's a big palace. She isn't fond of walking." I looked at his face and saw the amusement he was having at my expense now that disaster had been averted. But then he showed me that it hadn't been a mocking smile. "I must thank you," he said. "I'm impressed."

"I have to say I'm just surprised. I knew I had to try something, and military toys were the first thing that came into my mind."

"You were briefed well then. Indeed, you chose the only thing that can break through his stubbornness at times like this—military planes."

"But did you see his eyes? Don't you people know just from seeing him that—?"

"Shhh. It's not something to talk about here—not anywhere in Balrampur. You are just seeing how serious and difficult the situation is—why your government brought you in. And I must say, they certainly knew what they were doing when they sent for you."

"I don't know about that. My . . . session with him was a complete bust. He was completely indifferent to me."

"Oh, you think so?"

"You had to be there to see how it went."

"You don't think I was there . . . somewhere nearby?" I turned my head to him again to find he still was smiling. It was still a smile of amusement, but there also was something else in that smile. "He got hard, didn't he?" Adil said in a low, hoarse voice.

41

"He was hard before I arrived . . . he had already started—with that actress mistress of his."

"Ah, Aruna. Such a complication there. But who was he with when he ejaculated?"

"You seem to know."

"Yes, I do. And you did superbly."

He was still holding me in an embrace, and ever so briefly I thought that he was going to kiss me. But he didn't. He released me instead and continued talking in that calm, in-command tone he'd used since he entered the room.

"But we must save this discussion for later. You have promised the Rawal a plane ride, and he isn't likely to think of anything else until he gets his plane ride. We must be out in the motor court waiting for him when he wants to leave. You may have noticed; the gun was still in his hand when he left here."

I looked into his face again. The corners of his mouth were still turned up in the mirth position, but I knew he wasn't joking all that much.

"I don't know how you can do this day in and day out," I said.

"It has its rewards. And the challenges are worth not living like most of those in Balrampur do. I must say that thus far you've only seen the surface of life here. There is little choice to be made on living inside the palace grounds if you can. And I can assure you the inner workings of the palace are much more complex than this even. You will need all of your wits about you. I am pleased to see that you seem to have them in abundance—not to mention other alluring aspects of you that you have in abundance."

I rather liked the smile he gave me when he said that.

* * * *

"That's enough. We can go up now."

"I'm afraid not, Prince Bhadur Khan. In the palace your world is law, but here it's that man sitting in the flight building who tells us what we can do and when we can do it. You're an expert pilot; you know that you need to be thoroughly checked out on the Magnus before you fly this baby. One mistake and you're dead. What good would that do Balrampur?"

"I want to go up today."

"Then exchange seats with me, and I'll take you up. It will add checkout time and make it all that sooner that you can solo on the Magnus."

He was really being pretty reasonable about this considering what I knew he was capable of. I'd almost thought I had to hit the panic button to bring Roger Allard in on the problem, but when I called on the prince's professionalism he had responded.

"Tell you what, though," I said. "Here, let me show you how the manual settings of the aerial cameras work. I'll fly around Balrampur while we're up, and you can fire off some photos you've taken yourself that you can show around the palace by tomorrow evening. It will take a day for them to process the film at the consulate."

He was good at that, too—at taking aerial shots. We flew around the country and up and down the line of the Siwalik Range that separates Balrampur and other parts of India from Nepal. The prince was professional in everything he did in the air and was completely focused. It was almost as if he were two men—with not much more than one brain to share between them.

It also was a turn on for him. As we flew, I could see his flight suit tenting and his eyes slitting in pleasure. But the sexual arousal the prince obviously got from playing flyboy didn't completely obliterate everything else in his mind. I was to find that he hadn't forgotten about his wife at all. When we came down and were taxiing the plane, I heard him mutter, "I will kill her."

I said nothing.

"Flying was better today, but someday—soon—killing her will be better." I believed he meant it.

Exiting the plane, he turned to me and said in a gruff voice, "In the back of my limousine."

"I'm not supposed to go back to the palace, Prince. It's getting dark and I'm supposed to be in the consulate compound tonight . . . unless, of course, you wish for me to come back to the palace." I'd almost done it again. I hadn't been thinking fast enough and had stomped on my own crank. The storm clouds forming in his eyes telegraphed my mistake. We seemed such equals while we were in the air that I forgot that I was never to even hint a "no" to him elsewhere.

"OK, OK," I said before he could explode. "In the back of your limousine. As you wish, of course."

He was unzipping his flight suit as he entered the car behind me. Mir Yusaf Adil had been in the limo, and he exited by the door on the other side as I entered. The Rawal plopped in the center of the backseat and pushed me down on the floor of the limo between his knees. The limo remained stationary.

"The balls," he said.

His were the size of large walnuts, and I learned that he could moan in sex as, at his direction, I took them in turn in my mouth and sucked on them. He wouldn't let me touch his cock, which, as I surmised, had gotten hard while we were flying; he worked that himself. All he wanted me to do was suck his balls.

When he had come, he told me I could get out of the limo. Adil reentered when I exited, and they left me there to walk back to the flight building across the hot tarmac on my own.

* * * *

It had been an exhausting day, and I'd showered in my small studio apartment in the consulate compound, toweled off and stretched out on the bed with just the towel around me.

I was reading over the pilot's manual for the Magnus, making sure I was thoroughly briefed up on every aspect of that because I assumed that I wasn't going to be able to hold the prince off another day on getting into the pilot's seat. I heard the click of a key in the door lock. I barely had time to sit up on the edge of the bed when the door opened and Mir Yusaf Adil entered.

"What? How?"

"I told you that I worked closely with the consulate and, especially, with Roger Allard. You have had quite a day. I have followed most of it. I haven't had the opportunity to appropriately thank you for your services and your fast-thinking actions today. And it is easier for me to come to you here than in the palace."

He sat down on my bed beside me and took the manual out of my hand, closed it, and placed it on the nightstand.

"It's my job," I said. "You don't really have to—"

"Your body must be one big painful cramp."

I had to stifle a gasp as he touched my arm with his long, sensuous fingers and moved them up to my bicep and back down to my elbow, causing chills to run up my spine. If this was foreplay, he was very good at it.

"I entered the palace services as a masseur," he said. I hardly heard him, though, as there was a buzzing of arousal in my ears. "I bet my file with your Mr. Allard doesn't mention that."

"You must have been very good at it." My voice was low and husky. I was sorry I had spoken. I didn't want him to think I was this easy if he wanted me—and I couldn't bear the thought that he might not want me.

"I was. I am." I felt the loss of him taking his hand away from my arm but almost flinched when I felt his fingers touch me low on my belly. I looked down to see that he was unknotting the towel at my waist and slowly opening the towel and moving it aside. Of course I already was hard for him. I was embarrassed even though that wasn't rational—he'd already seen me naked.

He pulled his silk sherwani over his head. He was wearing a white cotton dhoti, knotted at his waist, underneath that. I almost laughed, as it reminded me of a diaper.

But I was too far gone in lust to laugh. His body was beautiful. Lithe, dark, and strongly muscled. And both sinuous and sensuous.

"Have you really come here just to give me a massage?" I was being brazen. I didn't want that to be the only reason he was here—and in that, I was rewarded.

"I'll do that, of course, but what I've really come here for is to fuck you. And at this point it is safer for me to do that outside the palace. If you wish to continue with me, I can make arrangements, of course, but that will take time, and I find I do not want to wait. You do want me to fuck you, don't you? I didn't misread your responses to me, I hope."

I gave him the only answer I was capable of giving him. I raised a leg, turned my torso toward him, and lowered my leg to behind his back so that he now sat between my thighs. I was in position for him to enter me if he wished. I was more than ready for that. His foreplay was pleasant, but I wanted him to make love to me. For a moment, I thought we would go straight to it, as he leaned over to me and took my lips with his in a kiss. When he sat back up, I saw his hand at the knot of his dhoti, and when he'd untied that and pushed the material away, I saw that no more foreplay was needed by him either.

But then he laughed and stood up from the bed. "Lay on your back," he said.

I groaned, and reached for his cock. But he brushed my hand away with another low laugh. "All in good time," he whispered. "It will happen, but it will be more enjoyable by the anticipation of it. You Americans are much too impulsive. Treasures are greater that are savored."

I laid full length on the bed on my back, as he had commanded. He had a bottle of lotion with him, and he expertly worked my muscles with the lotion, following that up with his tongue. I was moaning and sighing as his mouth came down over my cock. He had me turn over, and repeated his sensuous massage with his hands, followed by his tongue. When he mounted my hips with his pelvis I had been grinding my cock into the bed and had raised my buttocks instinctively. My channel was so open for him that he just slipped in and mined my channel deep in long, slow strokes. When he was close to climaxing, he reached under my belly and pulled me up on my knees. He laced my balls between the fingers of a hand at the root and when he ejaculated, he distended and squeezed my balls, and with a small cry I came too.

We lay stretched out along each other, everything touching that we could get to touch. It was the first real loving I'd had all day.

"That's one of the secrets with the prince," he murmured. I had to make him repeat it to make sure I'd understood him.

"What I did with your balls. The prince is a balls man."

"So I gathered. That was the only moaning I got from him today—other than the sheer joy he obviously felt in being in the sky. He moaned when I sucked his balls. He told me to suck his balls."

"What I did to you. If he gets too rough or you just want to bring it to a close, do that to his balls. Lace them through your fingers and extend them with a tug. He'll come immediately. And when he comes, he's finished. It doesn't mean that you didn't do well or he didn't find you arousing enough. When the Rawal comes, the Rawal is finished with sex. If the one servicing him displeases him, he won't just walk away. The person will know for sure that he has failed."

"I'll keep that in mind. So, this whole visit was to show me that technique?" I said it in jest, of course, but this whole palace intrigue situation had me off my pins. I wanted to know that I had pleased him. That he would fuck me again.

"No, this visit was because I couldn't keep my hands off you any longer, and it would have been awkward for the Rawal to find me fucking you in the corridor of his palace."

Nothing was said then for some time, as he had regained the strength of his cock, and we both wanted what he had to give me. Afterward, we both were spent, and I was pleased to find that he didn't want to just rise, dress, and leave; he wanted to hold me and to kiss my lips and my nipples.

"I need you to move into the palace."

"I'm not sure . . . I don't think Allard will—"

"Allard will give me whatever I need to keep the situation under control. That scene today . . . with the princess. It will become more serious."

"Surely it couldn't get any more serious than a bullet being fired."

"She's on the warpath because the Rawal is openly being seen with his mistress. The Rawalina doesn't want him. She just doesn't want not having him being flaunted in public."

"How will it get worse, then?"

"Aruna is pregnant. The prince has already said he wants to divorce the Rawalina and marry Aruna."

"But his mother, the Badshahrina. Isn't she Vimala's aunt? Didn't she arrange the marriage?"

"Precisely. You can see the complexity, can't you? I will want to introduce you to the Badshahrina soon. She is your country's best ally here in Balrampur. I believe she will need your help."

"I can't wait." But of course I could. I didn't want to get any more involved in palace intrigue than I could possibly help doing.

"Oh, and one more thing. Don't trust the Badshah's adviser, Ambedkar Sungar, in any matter. He is a nasty piece of work. Try not to antagonize him either"

"So I've already gathered," I responded.

"There are rumors he is working with Al-Qaeda, the Muslim terrorists."

I didn't respond to that. That seemed to be a theme that many wanted to get across to me.

"You are good for the Rawal, I think. Very good. And for the situation overall. So, you must move into the palace."

"Then you don't want . . . this? You said it would be difficult in the palace."

"I very much want this. I will find ways."

Then his hands started roaming my body again and I was lost to him once more, this time his mouth working my cock while his finger tips made love to my prostate.

After he had left, I heard the monitor in the overhead camera click on, and I looked up to see Roger Allard's stern-looking face filling the screen. Of course he'd seen the whole thing—or, at least, he would have ready access to a tape of what I and the Balrampur official had been doing in my room. He may not have seen it live, but it would all be on videotape. I certainly hoped Adil wasn't lying about having permission to have come here . . . and having done what he did.

"Roger. I didn't know he would . . . I didn't invite him."

"It's not that. That's fine. Good work. I need you to come over to the consulate—my office—immediately. We've got a situation on our hands."

As the monitor clicked off and I padded in for another quick shower before dressing in record time, I couldn't help but think that "a situation" was pretty much the norm for this tiny semiautonomous enclave.

Chapter Four

"Do you see what I see in these photos?"

"Let's see. No, I don't . . . but yes, yes, now I think I do. This looks like a rifle firing range and that area over there like an obstacle course."

"Yep, afraid that's what I see too."

I was standing and leaning over Roger Allard's desk in the station. He had a bunch of blown-up photographs strewn around on the top of his desk. Some of them were still slightly damp from the developer.

"But, what does that mean?" I asked.

"Nothing good, I'm afraid. It matches some other scattered intell we've been getting. It's been so buried in chaff and is so speculative, though, that we hadn't taken the time to check it out yet. We sure as hell will check it out now, though."

"OK, it looks like a low-scale training base. And the figures out on the courses have their heads covered with scarves. They certainly aren't garbed like Indians. So, it looks like an Arab setup. But where is it and what's the significance?"

Allard looked worried, and that worried me. "It looks like a lot of other training bases the Al-Qaeda or Al-Qaeda wannabe movements have tucked around in developing countries," he said. "The problem is that this one is here, in Balrampur, not far from the Nepal border. Which means not far from us—either the consulate or the palace. And it's not one of the known bases in our records. It might mean one of several things, none of them good for our business here. We could be a target—our airbase. The palace could even be a target. It could be directed toward Nepal too. But it's new and it's here and it's our headache. We found it and it's in our jurisdiction."

"Where did you get these photos? And how old are they?" I asked.

"You got them," Allard answered. "Or, more correctly, Prince Bhadur Khan got them. These are from the joy ride you took him on yesterday in the Magnus. He hit a gold mine on his first ride."

"And I've promised him photos for souvenirs."

"Not these particularly photos. Not to the prince. We've got plenty of other shots he'll like. He was good with the camera controls—no empty sky or cloud shots. But we have to keep this close hold until we can check the place out and see if we can neutralize it before they can get these terrorists trained up to do something we won't like."

"So, nobody outside the station gets told? We don't say anything to the government so they can bolster security?"

"Not now. Not yet. We'll slip the information to the government through Mir Yusaf Adil as soon as we can get a grasp on what it means ourselves. Incidentally, you've been called to the palace. Adil wants you to move in, and I told him that was fine with us."

"Uh, about Adil."

"That he was with you before I summoned you? Yeah, I have eyes and ears. Give him anything he wants. He's our main connection with the palace. And, for that matter, I suppose we should tell him something now. I want you to tell him there's a threat—that maybe they are training somewhere too close. Nothing more specific than that. But he needs to step up palace security as much as he can without alerting General Sungar or the Rawal. And I'd like permission to bring some of the Blackshield guys in. We can't have the place crawling with agents we can't disown. The Blackshield guys are mainly former Agency or Seal. We need to beef up security around the airfield—and I'd like to get some of our assets into the palace compound too."

"And you want me to cover all of that with Adil?" I asked, just to be sure.

"Yeah, and, Craig, I think Adil's going to hit you with some sort of outlandish scheme concerning the Badshahrina and Rawalina. If he does, he's discussed that with me too, and it's a go as far as I'm concerned. I don't think it will pan out, but he's hot to trot on the idea. Cooperating will keep him and the Badshahrina's faction quiet for a while. We gotta keep Adil and his team on our team."

I couldn't wait to hear what Adil's little scheme was all about. Allard looked a little embarrassed when he told me he endorsed it. It had to be something nasty. I'd yet to see Allard squeamish about just about anything.

* * * *

First things first. When I was taken back to the palace, it was me back to the Sports House while my luggage went on to the main palace. I was told I would be shown to my new quarters later but that now the Rawal wanted to look at the photography he'd shot from the Magnus the previous day. It was usually a three-day process for a turnaround on these photos, but Allard had wisely put an all-night rush on them. And a good thing he did too. I had told Allard I'd only promised them to the prince in an offhand way, and Allard had told me there was no offhand way with Bhadur Khan. I was still fucking up in fully understanding the totality of the prince's power over my side—and how short his fuse was. I had so much to learn and so little time in which to learn it.

Adil met me at the limousine, made sure that I was carrying a portfolio of the photographs, and started to escort me into the building.

"Can we talk a minute first, Kshatriyas?" I asked. "Out here, a bit away from the door, if we can?"

"Afraid of surveillance? Is it that sort of discussion?" He was smiling, but it was a sort of "smiling for the cameras" look, so I didn't think I needed to argue the point with him.

"Yes, I always assume surveillance. And, yes, it's that sort of discussion."

"You are right to do so. You never cease to please me. In every way imaginable." He was smiling "that smile" at me, and we were standing on the brown gravel drive well away from both the limousine and the door to the Sports House. The guards were studiously faced the other way. I almost reached out to touch him in a signal of endearment, but almost as if he sensed I would do that, he moved slightly away from me. And the warning look he gave me put me on my guard. I was learning, but perhaps not fast enough.

"There was evidence of something in photographs taken from the Magnus yesterday that I haven't brought to show the prince," I said. "Allard said I could tell you what they are, but not the location."

"What are they?"

"The prince unwittingly snapped shots of what looks like a terrorist training base while we were up in the Magnus yesterday, and we did not stray outside of Balrampur territory. I had no stomach for causing either the Indian or the Nepalese air force jets to be scrambled. Allard told me to tell you this because he wants permission to bring in professional civilian soldiers to protect against possible action from the camp and to neutralize it—both for your good and ours."

"Mercenaries? He wants to bring in mercenaries? American mercenaries?"

"Yes. Blackshield. They are highly trained. We would do what we could to keep them from being an embarrassment to you."

"Where is this terrorist training base and what is it targeted against?"

"We can't say what its purpose might be. And I'm afraid I can't tell you where the base is. I wasn't told myself. Allard says that's for your own good. We might choose to take it out, if we can do so without embarrassing your government. But if you do so, Allard says it should be based on information you formulated for yourself. He said that was in your best interest."

"This is a disturbing wrinkle," Adil said. "I will see what I can do about the request to let mercenaries in the country. None of these mercenaries could come inside the palace compound, of course. General Sungar wouldn't countenance that. And if there's a terrorist base nearby, I believe he already knows that. Causing Sungar any concern or suspicion might move up their action plan."

"Yes, Allard agrees with that."

"Come with me to the prince with your photographs. While you are in audience with him, I'll see what I can do about this matter. And then, after you have been to your quarters and dressed appropriately, we have an audience with the Badshahrina."

"The Badshahrina?"

"Yes, she wishes you to do something for her."

I walked the corridor toward the locker room with him, wondering just how convoluted my role in palace machinations was going to get.

The massage room was spacious, but it seemed less so because of all of the people milling around in it.

"Damn," I heard Adil mutter under his breath as we entered. "I didn't expect them to be here this soon."

But only I—and maybe the professional deaf and dumb uniformed guards at the doors—heard him, I'm sure. Outwardly, he was all smooth unction and smiles.

The centerpiece of the room, fittingly, was Prince Bhadur Khan, laying on his belly on a massage board, not even with a towel around him. A pouting Aruna was off to one side, being fanned by two middle-aged women in saris. The room was steamy and full of sunshine from a massive skylight overhead. Aruna was wearing her signature big-lens sunglasses. I couldn't keep myself from looking at the swell of her belly, wondering now how far along she was.

There was the masseur, of course, and assorted uniformed guards, but there also were three officious-looking men in their forties and fifties dressed in somber-colored, but expensively cut sherwanis. These men had briefcases and thick stacks of documents.

As Adil and I entered, though, the prince turned his face to us, sat up on the edge of the massage table, and waved the official-looking men away. They and the masseur backed out of the room in a low bow. The guards also receded into the wall paint.

"The aerial shots? You brought them?"

"Yes he did, of course," Adil answered, motioning me forward. And then he too backed out of the room, bowing, in the wake of the three officials.

"You took some really good photographs," I said, opening the portfolio I had brought with me. "Some great ones of the Sravasti area." I didn't mention the even better ones of a terrorist training camp that I hadn't brought.

We spent several minutes looking over the photos—the technology of which I could readily see aroused him—and then he commanded me to strip off my trousers and briefs.

He fucked me, bent over the massage table. Again, it seemed so impersonal and passionless that I wondered why he bothered. He thrust up in me in deep, swift strokes, and he arched my back up to him, without permitting me to touch his chest, by pulling my head back with his fist gripped in my hair.

When it was getting tedious for me, I remembered to reach back and lace his balls through the fingers of one of my hands and tug and squeeze. He didn't react badly to this; indeed, he widened his leg stance as if he wanted me to do it. He came, with merely an "umpf" sound, almost immediately.

He showed no resentment that I had gripped his balls, but, other than a slap on one of my butt cheeks when he finished, he showed no emotional reaction to the coupling. I hasten to call it coupling, though, as clinical and detached as it was.

All the while Aruna sat there and watched us through her sunglasses with a pouty, but otherwise inscrutable, look on her face.

Adil was back and the prince flicked one wrist at me to back away, which I did, almost into Adil's arms, while he waved a hand for a guard to come forward and take the portfolio of photographs. The masseur was also reentering the room, as if he had watched everything for the signal of being needed again—which undoubtedly was the case.

In the corridor, Adil tugged at my sleeve—I was awkwardly carrying my trousers and briefs in my arms and walking like a duck from the temporary stretching the prince had done of my channel—and pulled my ear closer to his mouth.

"You need to watch out for that Aruna," He whispered. "She is taken with you. But you must not fuck her unless the Rawal puts you in that position. He'll have you killed if you do."

"Aruna wants me?" I muttered in disbelief. She was almost as close to being a statue in my presence as the guards were. I couldn't imagine that she was "taken with" me, as Adil had put it. But of course I had fucked her already. So, who knows? This whole palace entourage seemed screwier than hell—and they certainly screwed a lot.

"And be careful when we see the Badshahrina too. She also has a roving eye."

Oh brother!

* * * *

"Come closer."

I sat on the Badshahrina's voluminous bed and leaned down so that she could run a bejeweled finger across my cheekbone. I tried to ignore that the fingers of the other hand had unbuttoned the top of my shirt and were discovering my nipples.

We had found her, after a nearly interminable walk through the maze-like corridors of the palace, in her bed, propped up on a mountain of colorful pillows, when Mir Yusaf Adil and I were ushered into her chamber. We had been told that she had a slight cold, but other than being under a coverlet, she was decked out and slathered up with cosmetics as if on the way to a ball.

She wasn't a bad-looking woman and didn't seem all that old, maybe her early fifties, I thought, burdening her with a few more years than she looked in consideration of the pampering she must receive. Her pale, white skin contrasted with her jet-black hair. If there was a flaw in her features, it was a slightly hooked nose, which I had also noticed on the otherwise flawless face of the Rawalina I had so briefly glimpsed recently at the Sports House.

"The Kshatriyas tells me that you have Persian blood."

"Yes, I do," I answered, although I shot a glance at Adil. He didn't know that from anything I'd said. "My mother is of Iranian descent, yes. My father is the usual American mix, though."

"That is good. That will work," she said, and then she went on to say, as if I would see it as an explanation for anything, "I am full-blooded Persian, as is my niece, Vimala, the Rawalina. Yes, I think this will do fine."

I didn't ask her what the hell that meant, but I did look up at Adil, who was standing not six feet from us. The guards and other attendants were all standing at least twenty feet away, and I did notice that both the Badshahrina and Adil had been speaking in low tones as if we were involved in a very private audience.

"Divorce is in the air, and very soon," Adil murmured to me as I searched his face for understanding. "It's coming even sooner than we had anticipated, I am afraid," he added. "Those three men with the Rawal when we attended him. They are the court lawyers. They have drawn up the necessary papers."

"But can that just happen at the Rawal's whim?" I asked. "Isn't the Rawalina the Badshahrina's niece? Wasn't the marriage sanctioned and sponsored by the Badshah? Can it be broken that easily?"

"Alas, the Rawal and his mother haven't spoken for some time. He was quite the dutiful son—not even balking at marrying the woman his mother had chosen for him. But the two clashed from almost the beginning. The Rawal can pick the basis for a divorce as he likes. The Rawalina cannot put up any kind of a defense. To speak ill of the Rawal would be an act of treason—lese majeste—even for a Rawalina."

"Ah, lese majeste," I repeated as if it was an argument killer—and in a country as traditional as Balrampur, I had to admit that it probably did stand as the last word.

"I have decided that I have failed with my son," the Badshahrina said with a sigh. But then she subsided and it was left to the Kshatriyas to fill in the blanks.

"The Badshahrina's hopes have now skipped a generation," he said.

"But if the Rawal divorces the Badshahrina's niece—"

"Precisely," Adil interjected. "And a divorce is imminent. The Rawalina must be with child before the divorce is finalized, or she won't be carrying the legitimate heir to the kingdom."

"But, if it's true that the Rawal and his wife haven't been intimate for—"

"Truth is in the hands of those in power. The key to power in Balrampur is the one who is Badshah."

"You have the Badshah already, though, I answered—and his heir, in the form of Bhadur Khan."

"At some point there is a succession. This is a delicate point, but if there is no direct grandson possibility, the options are limited. And there is always the possibility of what happened in nearby Nepal in recent years—an event that curtailed more than one generation of the succession."

"A mass assassination, you mean?" I asked in a whisper. It, indeed, hadn't been that long ago—just a decade—that a mad member of the royal house in Nepal had taken it upon himself to shorten the succession rankings by trimming the royal tree with an M16. But perhaps Adil hadn't heard me—and, upon reflection, I hoped he had not. I still had much to learn on keeping my mouth shut and my suspicions to myself.

In any event, Adil at least diplomatically continued his explanation without skipping a beat—just as if he hadn't heard me. "The Badshahrina wishes to have a legitimate grandson by her niece, the Rawalina, to have her chance of rolling the die."

"But . . ."

"It is what my niece, the Rawalina wants too," the Badshahrina suddenly spoke. "She has seen you. It actually was her idea."

If I hadn't understood before, I certainly understood now. Now the questioning of my ethnic background was making sense. I turned my face toward Adil, in near panic, almost hoping I'd see a "this is all a joke" expression in his face. But I didn't.

"It is in your country's interest too," he murmured. "Roger Allard has given the plan his sanction."

And so he had. He had told me as much himself.

What could I say or do? This was the horse that the United States had backed and I was pledged to do whatever it took to preserve and further U.S. interests.

"But there isn't really time," I said in a last-ditch effort to stave off this monstrous plot. I could think it was monstrous, of course. I couldn't say it was, though. I could only salute and do as instructed. Unless I could talk them out of it.

"We know the shortage of time. That is why I am taking you to the Rawalina's apartment in a few minutes—if the Badshahrina decides you are suitable," Adil said. "She is waiting."

"If the Badshahrina decides—?" I started to say. But Adil already was bowing and backwalking out of the room and the Badshahrina was already unraveling the parts of her sari and revealing pendulous breasts with nipples the size of silver dollar, and a thick thatch of black curly hair below her rounded belly. I had no question what was expected of me when she took my head between two plump bejeweled hands and pushed it down to her crotch.

"Aieee, you are so huge," she murmured when the same hands guided my cock to her cunt.

"I can manage it myself—"

But her passage muscles had already gripped my cock and were pulling it deep inside here. Her sighs and moans for the next twenty minutes signaled that I would be quite a satisfactory seed donor for her niece.

* * * *

I didn't fuck the Badshahrina as much as I was drained dry by a woman of considerable experience who, like her son, was intent solely on her own satisfaction.

71

When Adil came for me afterward, he had mercy on me and didn't take me immediately to be similarly tested by the Rawalina. He took me to the apartment he'd said would be assigned to me and permitted me to shower and put on a sherwani and rest for a bit to regain my strength.

I felt like a condemned man an hour later as Adil and I and a retinue of four guards silently stole through the marbled halls of the palace to a remote wing. With all of the intrigue that was in the air, I expected an armed party doing either the Rawal's or General Sungar's bidding to intercept us at any moment. As wary as Adil and our escorts were, I guessed that they were that way for the same reason.

But we reached the Rawalina's apartment unchallenged, and as I went through a succession of guarded doors, also unchallenged, the escorts, and then Adil himself, separating off as we moved deeper into the inner sanctum. Until there was just me and the Rawalina in a bed chamber. She was laying naked on the bed, with pouting lips on her face and another pouting set between her thighs. I could tell that she was irritated at having been made to wait. Her expression softened considerably, though, when, having appeared briefly n the chamber after saying he had been checking to ensure we were alone, Adil helped me pull the sherwani over my head and bowed out of the room carrying my robe and she saw me naked. Her eyes slitted. She opened her legs, and one of her hands moved to between her thighs.

The Rawalina was neither unattractive nor inexperienced, and it wasn't long until I was breeching that last inner sanctum with a hard staff and she was clutching my shoulders with her sharp claws and mewing and groaning and moaning and meeting each of my deep thrusts with a counterpunch of her generous-sized hips.

"Three times a day until I am sure I am quickened," she murmured in my ear as Adil stole into the room and helped me rise from her and was directing me to a bathroom off the bedroom with a separate entrance away from her chamber. I looked back, and she was smiling in a way that told me she didn't consider this secretive act as all necessity and no pleasure.

"This is the back passage to your quarters," Adil was saying to me fifteen minutes later as we settled in the suite of rooms being assigned to me. He had shown me two ways to approach the rooms. One was from the central core of the palace, not far from the Rawal's wing, where I could attend on him within five minutes, when called. The other way, via narrow, almost secret corridors, led directly into the bathroom off the Rawalina's bed chamber.

I could see that I was going to have to learn to deftly juggle my appointments for a while. It actually would be more of an issue than I thought it would be, though, as Adil apprised me of presently.

"When you have seen what you wish to see here in your formal quarters, I will show you where we will meet."

"We?"

"You and I. We cannot meet here in your quarters," he whispered, pointing up to the camera monitors in the corners of the room that made no apology or attempt to hide their presence. "And it would not be right for us to meet in my apartments either. My wives are there."

"Your wives?"

"Yes, wives." He leveled a stare at me that said that this now was a closed topic. "And we will go to the more private apartment now."

In stark contrast to both the Rawal and General Sungar, Mir Yusaf Adil was both an attentive and inventive lover. I had come twice under the ministrations of his gliding and probing hands and tongue before—with me whimpering and begging for the fuck. And when he did fuck me, he rarely did it the same way twice. That afternoon I found myself supporting my weight on the back of my neck and my shoulders on a thick Oriental carpet, with my buttocks and legs waving in the air, as he stood sideways between my thighs, holding my ankles in his hands in a stance that looked like he was a Nordic cross-country skier, and fucked down into my channel.

Contemplating the four couplings I had experienced that day and anticipating the nightly visit Adil said I would be making to the Rawalina, I almost hesitated to mention a need of my own—and of the station's. But I worked up the courage to ask him, as, rather than just leaving me after the fuck, he stretched out beside me and rocked my body in his embrace and kissed my nipples and neck.

"I have an operational need to go to the consulate—to my real job—daily."

"You need not worry about that," he whispered in my ear, the lobe of which he'd been playing with with his teeth. "Tomorrow I will introduce you to Colonel Agar."

"Colonel Agar?"

"Yes, he's the chief of the Rawalina's guard. He will be your constant companion while you are here, scheduling your days and nights. He will make sure you fit it all in—and especially that you fit the Rawalina in without the Rawal's or General Sungar's knowledge. We need Colonel Agar. And he will want to make use of your body too. Roger Allard of course knows this and has agreed to it."

"Oh, god," I murmured in almost a whimper. This changed to "Oh, God! Oh, Shit!" as Adil had become hard again and was already entering my channel once more, while he held my body prisoner in his strong embrace.

* * * *

It wasn't just the Rawalina I was working on impregnating now—or, rather that I was being worked by; neither woman stooped to pretend it was a love affair. For every twice I visited her, I was taken to fuck the Badshahrina once as well. And she was twice as taxing and draining as Vimala was. I had perpetual claw marks on my buttocks from her holding me inside her while her passage muscles milked me like I was a cow. And that is exactly how I felt about my couplings with her—she was the bull and I was the cow.

"I do believe that she is hedging her bets," Adil told me one evening. "She told me that she could produce another crown prince herself—one who would be more malleable than the one she has. But I had dismissed the idea. More the fool I, though. Many have been defeated in dismissing her."

"But could she possibly?" I asked in amazement.

76

"She is in her mid forties," he said—which surprised me. I had assessed her as older.

Not noticing my double take, Adil continued. "The Badshah has had several wives. Interestingly, she was the youngest and yet is the only surviving one. Something to mark well, I would think. While it would be suicide to let the Rawal know you are coupling with with his mother, I would not suggest that you deny her anything."

"I hardly have the opportunity," I answered. "I think I know now how young wives feel whose powerful older husbands keep them merely for breeding. She's all business when I arrive, and woe unto me if I don't arrive with my dick standing straight out. Does the Rawalina know?"

"I doubt it," Adil said. "And I would not suggest that you tell her. I wouldn't overestimate the affection and loyalty that either of those woman have for each other. If Vimala knew that her aunt was racing her for the use of your cock . . ."

Adil left the rest of that unsaid. We both shuddered at the prospect of it.

I was soon lost in my own use of Adil's cock anyway. All of this heterosexuality was draining on me.

"I'm just the royal joy stick," I murmured as Adil kissed my neck and stroked my cock.

"Not just that," he said with a low laugh. "You are the royal ass channel too."

I groaned. But, truth be known, I couldn't wait to have him inside me.

Chapter Five

"I don't know what the hell happened, but they're gone."

"Who's gone," I asked.

I had just arrived at Roger Allard's office in the consulate and he'd pulled me into the station's "Bubble"— the purpose-built room the innards of which sat on a floating platform and which was safe from electronic surveillance. Colonel Agar had turned out to be a genius at scheduling my time. I had a palace limo dedicated to my needs, although what I really needed was a pair of roller skates to scoot around the marble-floored palace corridors between the prince's apartments, the Rawalina's apartments, the Badshahrina's quarters, and Mir Yusaf Adil's private trysting room.

At least the colonel himself wasn't too demanding of my services. He bowed to the needs of everyone else for his slice of me—including my duties at the consulate—and was so tired at night from his own juggling act that more often than not he was asleep, holding me in an embrace, before he could get around to anything penetrating.

Although at reception at the consulate I'd been told that Allard had to see me immediately, when I got to his office, his secretary told me to wait a moment—that he had someone in the office with him.

That someone, I could see when she walked out of Allard's office, was a quite strikingly beautiful Indian-origin woman in a tailored pant suit and white blouse. She was tall and leggy and of the "I'm in charge variety." She looked me up and down, and I got the impression that she had done a total assessment in seconds, although I had no clue what the result of that assessment was. Her expression was one of aloofness, amusement, and disdain all rolled into one. I chose not to entertain the idea that she was dismissing me; her smirk was really rather challenging, and with the recent practice I'd had with the palace women, I was beginning to include the stray woman in my interests.

She sailed on by me—I couldn't see whether it was toward the elevator down to reception or back into the bowels of the station; neither did I see if she was badged or not—and Allard took my arm and led me toward the Bubble.

"Who's gone?" I asked again. I wondered if Allard's consternation had to do with the woman I'd just seen—and perhaps because I had seen her. But he didn't say anything to dispel my wonder; he didn't even tell me who she was. I didn't ask. Every day in every way I was learning how to do this Indian-style spy stuff better. I'd ask around in the office later.

"The training camp. It's gone. We sent the Magnus out again to reconfirm its location and nothing was there this time. So, we sent it right back out to take more exacting photos, and there was evidence that a camp and the training courses had been there, but they are gone now."

"And no reports of terrorist activities anywhere?"

"None. You didn't mention this to General Sungar, did you?"

"No, of course not. You told me not to—and I haven't seen General Sungar since the day the Rawalina tangled with Bhadur Khan."

"Mir Yusaf Adil says he'll get permissions in order for the Blackshield contingent, but I have news for him— but news I won't tell him. They are already on their way."

"So, what do you want me to do? Go back to the palace? Go up in the Magnus for another run?"

"I received notification the prince is coming today to fly the Magnus. I suggest that you give him a thrill and let him pilot and that you fire off all the photos you can for as far out from here as possible. There were men on the ground in the shots he took the other day. They must have gone somewhere. If we can find out where, maybe we can discern what their target is."

The Rawal couldn't have been more pleased that I was going to let him drive. I'd told him earlier that he'd need at least one more day as copilot, and although he hadn't been happy, he had acceded to my declaration. It was interesting that in all things but military duties, the Rawal was a spoiled, stubborn, demanding man, but that when it came to operating a piece of military equipment, he followed the rules explicitly. It's probably what had kept him alive through many years of training in on exotic military systems. This most likely was a bit chagrining to some factions within the Balrampur palace cliques that would probably be pleased to be free of their lunatic heir apparent.

Bhadur Khan returned to demanding and driving after we'd landed, and I was told, once again, to step into the back seat of his limo. I rolled and sucked his balls as he sat in the center of the backseat, his head arched back on the headrest and moaning quietly and working his cock himself. This time rather than coming when I tugged on and squeezed his balls, he lifted me with strong hands at my waist before I could do that and sat me on his cock. He growled when I placed my palms on his chest, and I immediately raised my hands to grasp handles in the ceiling of the limo. He still didn't want me to touch him. I leveraged the soles of my feet off the floor of the car to rise and fall on his cock as he did his part, controlling the rhythm, by lifting and lowering me at my waist and thrusting up into me at a counter rhythm pace.

After he came, he held me there, motionless for a moment, and whispered, "I have been told that you have been seen in the corridors of Vimala's, the Rawalina's, wing. You haven't been attending her, have you?"

"The Rawalina lives in the palace?" I asked, feigning surprise. "I would have thought she would be someplace else." God, I hope you haven't heard about your mother was my next thought.

"What are we to do to make you remember what is wanted from you, what your place is?"

I realized that this was a rhetorical question, because although he'd had me suck his balls in the limo and left me on the tarmac the first time, this time we had had our sex while the limousine was on the move. When he'd asked that question, we had arrived in the motor court of the palace, and the two burly guards who opened the doors on either side of the vehicle when the limousine stopped . . . were naked.

"Remember who you are here for," the Rawal said in a calm voice as he was handed out of the limo. And as he emerged, the two guards entered from either side. They both had condoms on erect cocks, so no time was wasted in my asking what they were up to or in one taking up the center-seat position the Rawal had vacated and pulling me into his lap and onto his cock, facing the front of the limousine. The other guard went between my legs and grabbed my ankles. He spread and raised my legs until my feet were leveraging off the ceiling of the vehicle, while the guard under me tipped my body back and the one crouched

84

between my legs and grunted as he worked his cock inside me on top of that of that of the other guard.

It was a rough double fuck, as I'm sure they were told to do. And I could tell that they had worked together in this way before. I did all of the begging and sobbing and pleading and yelling that I thought was appropriate for the occasion, but the truth of the matter was that I'd been doubled before—and by guys better equipped than this. I sort of enjoyed it. But I certainly didn't let the guards know that. They were young, handsome, toned brutes, which seemed to be a requirement to be in the palace guard.

When I got tired of the play, I feigned unconsciousness, and they stopped and carried me into the palace and to my apartment, where a very worried Colonel Agar was standing and wringing his hands, obviously worried about me being off schedule. It was time for my nooner with the Rawalina.

And I would have been just as happy to skip that, but it was my channel that had been punished, not my cock, so the colonel whisked me away as soon as I'd showered and donned a sherwani over a somewhat bruised body. As we padded down the hall, I told him that someone was informing the Rawal of my visits to the Rawalina, but he said we would just be more careful—and that the visits shouldn't be necessary for too much longer. If seven fuckings during her high ovulation times hadn't taken effect, the plan probably wasn't going to work anyway.

"Eleven," I said.

"Eleven?"

"I gave her seed more than once four times. But who's counting?"

Later that evening, I was given more reason why I shouldn't have to visit the Rawalina anymore.

I was summoned to the grand audience room. As far as I could see nearly everyone in the palace had been summoned—with the exception, of course of the Rawalina and the Rawal's mother, the Badshahrina. As I entered the room and fanned to the left to stand as unnoticed as possible—although within striking distance of Colonel Agar—I notice that the Rawal was standing in front of his father's throne and Aruna, in a white sari but without sunglasses, was standing in front of the Badshahrina's throne but on the bottom step of three up to the throne platform. General Sungar, a great look of satisfaction on his face, was standing on the floor next to Aruna. And Mir Yusaf Adil was standing on the floor beside the Rawal. He had a weak, brave smile on his face. But he was white as a sheet.

Aruna wasn't showing her pregnancy yet. Her belly was a bit distended, but was only reaching the roundness of what any first-rate belly dancer would have. I could see the shape and shading of the ruby naval plug through the white silk of her sari.

It came as a great surprise—but probably shouldn't have—when General Sungar announced that what we had been summoned to was the marriage ceremony between Prince Bhadur Khan and the new Rawalina, Aruna.

Following a brief announcement that the former Rawalina, Vimala, had been divorced earlier in the day, the wedding ceremony was quick and efficient and was followed by servants walking around with flutes of champagne and finger foods for all. No one approached the wedding party, nor was there any indication they were expected to—or would be permitted to. A revelation for at least me dropped during the ceremony when the family of Aruna was called forth to declare her suitability for marriage—which, amusingly, included declaration of her virginity—and General Sungar, only then identified to me as her uncle, stepped forward to do the honors and tell the expected lies.

General Sungar had hastened out as soon as the ceremony was over. And almost as quickly as he left, he had returned and come over to where I stood beside Colonel Agar.

"Where is she?" he hissed at Agar in low enough tones that I was probably the only one other than the colonel who had heard him. Everyone else around was studiously pretending like General Sungar wasn't even there. No one in their right mind wanted to come to the attention of General Sungar.

"She?" Agar answered, a look of innocence on his face.

"Vimala. You are her head of security. Where has she gone?"

Agar looked worried now, and it didn't appear to me that he was faking.

"I went to the Badshahrina," Sungar growled, "And she just smiled and said Vimala had gone into seclusion, because . . . because she was pregnant. With the Rawal's son."

The words came out like lashes, and Agar took them that way. This must have convinced Sungar that Agar wasn't holding anything back and that it was a waste of the general's time under these circumstances to dally here. He turned and gave me an angry, piercing look that made me want to shrivel into the marble wall, and then he turned and went directly to the prince.

The celebration was over immediately. The Rawal wheeled around and left through a door behind the thrones and everyone else in the hall evaporated.

They didn't all go, though, before Aruna moved and I saw the pair of ladies in waiting who had been standing behind her. My jaw dropped. One of them was the young woman I'd seen coming out of Roger Allard's office that morning.

Chapter Six

I was confined to my rooms for nearly two weeks after that, under a cloud for possibly having a part in the disappearance of Vimala, the former Rawalina. Colonel Agar had disappeared from my side, and everyone I asked about his absence just gave me a blank stare. It was as if he'd never existed at all—which I assumed was the normal way of taking care of people here who had lost their usefulness for the royals. I feared he might be below ground even because he had been Vimala's security chief and was revealed to have been spending the nights with me, which probably was a double whammy in the eyes of the prince. Worse, Mir Yusaf Adil wasn't visiting me either. I wondered if he had become another nonperson in the palace. If so, my own position was more precarious than ever before.

Roger Allard was let in after a week and told me he'd agreed to my confinement here as long as I came to no harm.

"The United States does look after its diplomats."

"Thanks so much," I responded somewhat acidly. "Why doesn't he just release me, then, and I can fly out of here?"

"He says he wants to fly the Magnus again, and I told him you were the only one I'd let him go up with. And there's the other matter."

"The other matter?"

"I understand he wants to enjoy you some more."

"And as long as there's the slightest chance—"

"Yes, I'm afraid so. Our assignment is still our assignment. Keep the prince happy and neutralized."

"What has happened to Adil?"

"That I don't know," Allard answered. And at this, I thought he looked a little concerned. Like maybe he was more concerned for Adil than for me. But I guess that was natural.

"Have we lost our leverage in the palace, then?" I asked.

"Not altogether. We have other assets. There's still you, of course. If the Rawal calls for you, I suggest you try to get back into his good graces. But we have other assets too."

"That woman I saw at the station the last time I was in? The one I saw playing lady-in-waiting to Aruna at the wedding?"

"Noticed that, did you? Let's just say we have other assets in place. But that's not why I came to see you today."

"Oh, I thought you wanted to be sure I wasn't strung up in a torture chamber somewhere—after a week of not knowing, of course."

"I've arranged for you to have the run of the palace compound again."

"That's comforting. I'm glad you're looking after my personal welfare."

"Yes, well, I've done that because there's a job I want you to do here later this evening. A diversion is going to be created that will focus attention here in the palace. While that's going on, I want you to go to the stables, as if after your confinement you want outdoor exercise, and to take a horse and ride to the place I have marked on a map of the palace compound."

Allard unfolded a map, which showed the walled palace compound to be a couple of hundred acres, the fringes of it wooded.

"And?" I asked.

"You should stay inside the tree line, but there's something we need visual verification of."

"You found where the terrorist unit went after they pulled up stakes, haven't you?"

"Yes, we think so. We think they are here, inside the palace compound itself. If you can verify that this is the case, we'll send in the Blackshield men during the night to sort the terrorists out. The permissions never came in from Adil, but if the terrorists have moved here, we want to neutralize them. And we do think they are here."

"And the diversion here in the palace?"

"You'll recognize it when you hear it. Just be somewhere around the throne room at about seven this evening."

"And in the meantime?"

"I asked the prince when I saw him just now if he wanted to go up in the Magnus this afternoon. I was working at putting you back in his good graces. But he said he had something else planned for this afternoon—that included you. So, I guess you'll be busy this afternoon—at least I hope it means he wants you again. Indications are that he's either forgiven or forgotten your connection with Vimala. Otherwise, he probably wouldn't have agreed to let you move around the palace again. And, here, I'm leaving you with this miniaturized satellite radio. Whatever you find, call me on this as early tonight as you can. Hide it well until then. And buck up. If everything goes well, we'll be pulling you out tomorrow. The Rawal says he definitely wants to drive the Magnus tomorrow. We'll make sure you get pulled back then. We'll think of a way to keep you from being pulled into his car when he leaves."

Allard stood and handed me the radio, and I slipped it into the secret lining compartment of my duffel bag.

"I'll have to shower and puff myself up," I said, with a sigh. The sigh was for effect. I needed sex; I'd been confined for a week. The prince's sex would do just fine.

Later I was to remember with regret that crack I'd made about torture chambers, though.

* * * *

The call came shortly after Allard left me. And it came in the form of four uniformed guards who were obviously there to ensure that I accepted the invitation to be in Prince Bhadur Khan's presence.

That was where the torture chamber idea came into play. I found that the palace had a dungeon a good three stories below ground level, all dolled out with vaulted stone ceiling and columns and stone walls and floor. And play equipment.

A figure was hanging from chains facing the wall when I was brought into the chamber. My first horrific thought was that it was Adil—but the figure was meatier than the lithe palace adviser was. The light was too dim to discern more than that during the time it took my guards to strip the sherwani off me as well as my briefs, which were the only other piece of clothing I'd been wearing, and to cuff one of my wrists into a manacle attached to a strong chain that was attached to the wall.

Upon further scrutiny, the figure looked like Prince Bhadur Khan, but that's hardly the position I'd ever have thought to see him in.

My escorts evaporated from behind me as the near-naked figure of General Ambedkar Sungar strode out from behind a stone pillar. He only wore a white dhoti around his waist and he held a scourging whip in his hand.

That's when I saw the welts already on the prince's back. Indeed, it was the prince, I now could see. The welts were just reddened stripped areas at this point.

As I watched, Sungar began to flick the scourge against the prince's back, which was bringing forth moans and groans from Bhadur Khan. They weren't groans of pain; they were sounds of sexual arousal such as I'd never heard from him in either his sex with me alone or in concert with Aruna. The general wasn't exactly punishing him, but the harder and faster he flicked the scourge, the deeper, more guttural the prince's groans were.

I hadn't realized that this could turn me on as well, but the sounds of passion that the prince was making affected me as well, and I was stroking my cock with my free hand.

After a bit, I heard the gloriously ominous command from the prince's lips. "Bring him to me."

General Sungar came over to me, uncuffed my wrist, and dragged me over to the wall. The instructions from Allard kept running through my brain: Make both of them happy; give them whatever they want. Return to the prince's good graces.

I found that there was an iron ring in the wall between the two that the Rawal's hands were chained to.

Sungar cuffed my wrists together and hung me from this ring, facing the prince. Then the general reached down and took each of my ankles, one by one, and hooked my legs over the prince's shoulders. He cuffed these with a chain linking them that prevented me from lowering my legs from that position. I didn't have the leverage or strength to raise both legs so that I could clear the prince's head with the chain.

The general then positioned the Rawal's cock between my butt cheeks. When the prince thrust inside me and started mining my channel, the general resumed his scourging of the prince's back, which I felt in the thickening and lengthening and more frenetic thrusting of the prince's cock inside me. This—this military discipline and cruelty— was the key to the prince's arousal.

I looked into the prince's face, which was drowned in lust and wanting, and it was the prince who brought his lips to mine and possessively took my mouth with his, thrusting his tongue inside and face-fucking me with it. He was making animalistic noises as Sungar scourge him, and when the prince let me up for air, his lips and teeth went down to my nipples. He punished me there, laughing and grunting at my moans and whimpering.

I heard the prince cry out and felt him flinch, and then he seemed to have lost his rhythm. But there was another rhythm, something else moving him, forcing his cock deep inside me and then relaxing and thrusting again. I opened my eyes and saw Sungar's huge hands spread on the prince's chest, his thumbs on the prince's erect nipples—and his chin resting on the prince's shoulder. Sungar was fucking Bhadur Khan who was fucking me—but only briefly, because I felt Bhadur Khan shoot his load inside me. He was moaning softly and Sungar was making a growly sort of laugh as his hand slid down the prince's torso and wrapped itself around my cock.

The Rawal just stood there suspended between me and the general, his cock inside me, still hard as a rock and gasping and grunting more passionately than he ever had done for me before, while Sungar finished getting both himself and me off.

I heard the prince utter a hoarse, "Unchain us both," and then we were both free, but Bhadur Khan was dragging me over to a cot in the corner and sitting down on that and forcing me on my knees between his spread thighs and my head down to his balls. I gave the orbs the suck I knew he enjoyed, while the general came up behind me, grabbed my waist in his hands, pulled me up on my knees, straddled my hips, and thrust inside me.

Sungar was humping me hard when the prince growled a "Me!" And then it was just me and the prince rolling around on the cot, with him trying to meld with me at every point—a real shock from his earlier behavior—and pumping me to beat the band.

They left me there when they were done, and I just lay there and moaned for several minutes.

Now I knew that it took a little discipline to really turn the prince on. Why was I not surprised. I remembered that the prince had been sent to a strict military school in England for his early schooling. It didn't take much imagination to figure out the lasting effect that experience had had on him. I told myself that I needed to upbraid Allard on this if I should survive this assignment. Somebody hadn't done their homework well enough concerning why the prince was as he was. It all seemed to make sense to me now. It wasn't really me they should have sent here. They should have sent a dominating controller and physical disciplinarian.

* * * *

I took my dinner early in my apartment after showering and taking a nap to regain my strength and composure.

Shortly before seven, I went to my door and tested it. The guards were gone, and no one was there to try to stop me from wandering. I had changed into brown and green riding gear from the wardrobe that had been provided the day after I'd first arrived here and padded down the corridor toward the throne room with my riding boots under my arm.

Allard had been right. It looked like everyone in the palace was drawn toward screeching I heard coming from the throne room. It was the voice of a woman, and she was so angry that I had trouble at first picking out her words. But once she started screaming, "fucking that bitch," I got the gist of it. And I also began piecing the situation together. It was déjà vu all over again. I hoped the prince didn't have a handgun with him as he did the day the then-Rawalina, Vimala, had upbraided him for having a mistress on the side. I would be interested in knowing how Roger Allard knew this was going to be happening at this moment.

The crowd huddled near the door into the throne room parted long enough for me to step forward and see four figures. The prince was standing in front of his father's throne, arms crossed, and looking irritated and haughty. Aruna was pacing the floor in front of him, dividing her attention between him and a worried-looking General Sungar, who was standing on one side of the throne dais, and . . . the lady-in-waiting I had first seen coming out of Roger Allard office at the station, was standing on the other side of the throne dais and, if anything, looking saucy and rather amused. She certainly didn't seem afraid of Aruna, who was charging her with being the Rawal's mistress.

At least who this woman was and why I'd seen her in the station was making sense now.

A lot of changing for just two weeks, I thought. But I also thought that this marriage to Aruna would probably end in one of the shortest ones on record, that the saucy lady-in-waiting had likely cooked it all up to give me time to accomplish the mission Allard had set for me, and that I better, literally, get on my high horse.

There were grooms at the stable, but they helped me with anything I wanted. It was only the inner palace staff that seemed to keep a running score on who was temporarily in and who was out.

I rode toward the quadrant of the compound Allard had told me to check out as directly and quickly as I thought I could without seeming to be on the mission that I actually was on. As I drew close to the northwest sector of the compound, I entered a copse of trees, dismounted, and tied my horse's reins to a low-lying branch. Then I moved as stealthily as I could to the other side of the stand of trees and peeked between the trunks of a twin-trunked tree.

What I saw was a meadow, depressed in a curve like a shallow mixing bowl with trees all around it. It wasn't a small area, and yet the first impression I got of what I was seeing was of a lake with lapping waves. But the waves weren't blue. They were a brown and green camouflage tenting and they covered a large area to one side of the meadow, with an obstacle course and what looked like an entrance into a firing bunker at the other end of the meadow. It was the breeze wafting through the depression that made the camouflage tenting wave like that. I was surprised that the camp had been picked out of the photographs the Magnus had taken.

It was twilight, and men in camouflaged fatigues and head scarves—all seemingly of Middle Eastern or South Asian origin—were creeping out of the sea of tenting and into the obstacle course. This apparently was the hour of safety for training routines.

Three men in sherwanis were standing at the edge of the tented area, prepared to watch the terrorists—for that's what they surely were, the disappearing terrorist training unit—preparing to go through their paces. The three men had their backs to me, but I moved my foot and must of snapped a twig, because one of the men, the tallest one, looked around. He didn't appear to pick me out of the surrounding forest, but I clearly saw his face before I ducked for cover.

It was the Kshatriyas, Mir Yusaf Adil. I could hardly stifle my gasp at sudden realization of everything that was happening here. All of this misdirection toward General Sungar as being a connection to Al-Qaeda. I was willing to bet that the origin of all this speculation had been Adil— and that Allard had believed anything Adil hinted to him, thinking that it was the Kshatriyas that the station had in its pocket. I had to get back to the palace and use the miniature satellite radio to let Allard know both that the terrorist unit was where he thought it was and that Mir Yusaf Adil wasn't who Allard thought he was.

I turned the horse back to the stable hands without a hitch, but as I was moving toward the palace, I saw lines of uniformed guards brandishing lighted torches streaming out of the palace entrances and into the grounds. I had no way of being sure, but chances were good that they were looking for me.

I was standing by the swimming pool near the Sports House at that point, so I just redirected my steps and headed for one of the doors into the Sports House. As I approached the door, the lady-in-waiting, or possibly the prince's new mistress or Roger Allard's agent—or, most likely, all three—emerged from the shadows and put her hand on my sleeve.

"My name as Devasree," she whispered. "I am one of Roger's NOCs," which told me that she was one of the chief of station's in-country assets. "Are they there or not? The terrorist band."

"Yes, they're there. But you also need to tell—"

"Shhh. Guards are there, over by the pool. They are looking for General Sungar and Aruna. We mustn't be seen together."

With that, she had retreated back into the shadows before I could say anything about Adil. I crouched down, spun through one of the doors into the Sports House, and moved as quickly and quietly as I could down the corridors.

I was completely lost—at least until I found the locker room. I entered that. I could hear steps outside in the corridor where I'd just been, though, so I went through a door at the back of the locker room. All I could think of was to get back into the palace proper unnoticed and find my way to my apartment to message Roger and then to stay put, playing the innocent and taking it from there.

I went through a series of service rooms that were getting smaller and smaller until I entered another large room that had a whole line of washers and dryers in it. I was circling the banks of those when another door opened and General Sungar entered the room.

"Good. I have need of you."

"General. The guards. I understand they are looking for you."

"I understand that as well. Come."

I hesitated for a moment. I was suddenly lost concerning who was an ally and who wasn't. If Adil wasn't true to U.S. interests, perhaps General Sungar was.

I never resolved that conundrum, but Sungar didn't wait for me to. He evaporated the distance between us in three long strides and closed the vice of his fist over my wrist and wrenched me toward the door he'd entered by.

The guidance not to antagonize either the prince of the general rang through my brain from the instructions Allard had given me. I couldn't have broken away from him if I had wanted to, but my instructions seemed to be clear on not fighting him.

We were outside. Not in the formal entrance motor court for the Sports House, but in some side service motor court. A beat-up old sedan was half hidden under a cascading willow tree. There was a driver in front, and I could see Aruna in the back, which I could tell by the flash of her jewelry and the metallic-material sari I'd seen her wearing earlier when she was tongue-lashing the prince.

"I need a pilot," the general muttered as he manhandled me toward the car and both the front and rear doors on the passenger side popped open. "And you're just the pilot I need."

Chapter Seven

The fleeing General Sungar and his niece, the increasingly rotund Rawalina, Aruna, didn't need a pilot for very long, and Sungar almost made a nasty point of this after I no longer was needed in that role. If I hadn't been in such a precarious predicament, though, I might have been amused by this musical chairs version of revolving and fleeing Rawalinas.

The general's nondescript car drove us to a military base the size of a postage stamp with an air strip not much bigger. He commandeered an old Cessna 172, which might have been the mainstay of the Balrampur Air Force for all I knew. I flew him and his niece to New Delhi, where it seems the Balrampur royal family had a much nicer Boeing

707 stashed away. They also had a brace of pilots and a couple of air stewards who looked more like heavyweight fighters on retainer there.

When we climbed out of the Cessna and I saw that the Boeing, distinguished by the Balrampur flag on its tail, was revving up its engines nearby without any help from me, I let Sungar and his niece start off without me and when they turned, I waved, told them to have a nice trip, and let them know they need not worry about me. I could find my own way back, I said.

The general and a nasty-looking pistol disagreed with me, and I quickly learned that I'd be taking the next flight with them, wherever that was.

It turned out that what was intended was that I would only be half right.

When I was herded aboard the 707 and through a seating compartment back to one with four single beds jammed against the fuselage, two to each side. I was pushed down on one of these on my back and, at Sungar's instructions, the two stewards forced my hands above my head and handcuffed me to the headboard railing. He and his henchmen left me there and went forward until we'd taken off.

I had no idea where we were flying, and I equally didn't know why I was being treated like this. I'd even tried to tell General Sungar as we were flying into New Delhi that I thought my boss at the U.S. consulate, Roger Allard, might have had an incorrect impression of him—especially in relationship to the Kshatriyas, Mir Yusaf Adil, and if only he'd let me contact Allard . . .

But Sungar was having nothing of that, and he was nothing but gruff and rough with me right up to and including trussing me up in the bedroom compartment of the 707.

I thought for a while that they had forgotten me, and then for a while that I was getting more than enough attention—and then, briefly, that I was getting entirely too much attention.

After we'd been in the air for an hour or more, the door from the seating compartment slid open and someone entered the sleeping section. The lights weren't turned on so I didn't know who it was until she got close enough for me to figure it must be Aruna from the strong whiff of perfume I got. I didn't tag the general as the perfume kind, so mine wasn't particularly a brilliant deduction.

Aruna used me as her toy gear shift, and I would have complained if I wasn't enjoying it. She unzipped me and played with my cock until it was standing at rigid attention, and then she hoisted up her sari around her waist and straddled my pelvis and rode me until I gave her an internal bathing. That seemed to satisfy her, and she simply climbed off me and left me in the dark.

The attention I got not long after that was a bit much, though, and it really choked me up. General Sungar flipped on the light when he came in. And he didn't just unzip me and slip what he wanted to play with out of my trousers. He stripped me of my trousers and unbuttoned my shirt and pushed that up over my head and up my arms. He'd had a multitailed black leather short whip with him ever since he'd accosted me in the palace Sports House laundry room, and he brought that into the sleeping compartment with him.

Whereas Aruna had wanted my cock, the general wanted my ass channel. He rolled me over on the bed so that I was on my belly, and then he mounted me from behind, hard and deep. While he rode my ass, he switched my bare back and thighs with ever-sharper flicks of the whip.

I gave him the noises I knew he wanted to hear— and I would have given them to him anyway. I didn't mind the fucking one bit, but the lashing was making me worried and was beginning to hurt, as it became more frenzied. I thought this was the worst of it, but I wouldn't have complained so much if he hadn't moved into another gear. He no longer was lashing me with the whip, but he had wrapped it around my throat and arched my head up toward him as he pumped my channel with his cock.

I gagged and fought for breath, feeling that he was timing his ejaculation for my own demise. And we were quite close to that point, when I heard the door to the seating compartment whoosh open and Aruna's voice barely cutting through the fog I was sinking into from the choking.

"Uncle. I think you need to come forward immediately—and not continue that. The pilot has received an important communication. It's about the American. You really must stop that. We're undone if you—"

"In . . . a . . . minute. I understand. I don't finish him—yet. Go. close the door." The general's voice was hoarse and full of arousal. He released the whip around my throat, and I took air in in great gasps and coughs. He rode me for less than a minute longer before he came. Then, with a mutter of "I'll be back," he was gone.

He didn't come back, however. In about a half hour, the two stewards came in. One held a gun on me while the other one released me and let me go into the head and clean myself up, do what I needed to do in relief of my systems, and even take a shower in the miniscule cubicle devoted to that. My briefs, trousers, and shirt were returned to me, somehow miraculously straightened of wrinkles, and I was led into the seating compartment, where I was seated on the back row, a considerable distance from where the general and the Rawalina of the moment were sitting. I was handcuffed by one of my wrists again to a handle on the fuselage, but I otherwise was fed and pampered by the stewards as well as any passenger in a private Boeing 707 could wish to be.

I was told to let the stewards know if I needed to visit the facilities again, and when I did so, I once more was marched back by the two stewards, with one holding a gun and exhibiting as someone who knew how to use it.

I slept for I don't know how long and when I woke, it was early morning outside the plane window and we were flying over snow-capped mountains that looked quite familiar to me. We also were descending. I gauged we were going to land in either Switzerland or Germany's Bavaria.

* * * *

"I trust you have been treated well."

"Most of the time, Roger," I answered, "although at one point I was getting such close attention that I got all choked up about it."

"Yes, I gather. But the communications I initiated came in time, I understand."

"Close enough."

It had been a long ride in the limousine from the airport. I hadn't gotten close enough to a terminal to have a precise idea where we were. The jet was parked on an apron far away from the terminal area, and the car was waiting for us on the tarmac nearby when the flight stairs had been hooked up to the Boeing's door. The limousine ride had been almost entirely uphill. The buildings sliding by could have equally been quaint Swiss chalets or quaint Bavarian chalets. The expression on the general's face signaled that I wasn't to ask him any "where" or "why" questions, and the bored expression on Aruna's face, now covered by her trademark big-lens sunglasses told me that she neither cared nor knew anything about "where" or "why" either.

When the limousine pulled up in a precariously small motor court beside a massive chalet barely hanging on the side of an alp overlooking a lake—and maybe Zurich?—I was escorted in one direction, around the down slope side

113

of the house, and the general and Aruna went directly into the building.

When I saw the two men, bundled in fur coats, sitting at a patio table on a deck overlooking a gorgeous view down into the valley, I probably shouldn't have been surprised—I probably should have figured out how and why General Sungar's little snuff scene had been interrupted, but I still was surprised enough to have to lift my jaw off the floor.

Sitting with a rotund old Indian-looking man was Roger Allard. As I walked toward the table, keeping an eye on Roger's benign smile, a servant came up behind me and wrapped me in a fur coat of my own.

When I reached the table, the old man said, "You may sit." And he said it in such a way that it dawned on me exactly who he was.

"Craig, may I introduce you to the Badshah of Shwetambar, Balrampur's ruler," Roger said, as he pulled out a chair for me to sit.

"So I gather," I murmured.

"We were just reviewing the state of play in Balrampur, and the Badshah wanted to convey his appreciation to you for the help you've been."

"The help I've been," I repeated dumbly.

"Yes. Devasree got your message to me and, the Badshah having extended his agreement, the friends we brought in temporarily—all gone from Balrampur now, of course—managed to clean up that little infestation in the palace garden."

"I need to tell you. Mir Yusaf Adil . . ."

"Ah, yes. We found him with his friends. We've taken care of that. Rather an embarrassment for me. One we needn't dwell on, though."

"Of course not," I agreed.

"We have other contingencies."

"Apparently so," I agreed. "Devasree?"

"Yes, for one. I believe she's already installed as the new Rawalina."

"More permanently that the last few, I hope," I said.

"She's a resourceful woman. And she will have help."

"Oh?"

"Yes. One of the Blackshield men. He seemed just perfect to step into both your and General Sungar's shoes as a special friend to Prince Bhadur Khan. I'm sure we can keep the Rawal quite happy from here on out."

"I hope he comes with a whip and a bark."

115

"He does, yes. We thank you for helping us to tune up what was needed in that department."

"We?"

"Oh, the Badshah and the U.S. government, of course." I looked over to the Badshah and he beamed at me as he bit into a peach. I could have sworn he winked. I certainly hoped I wasn't his type.

"No other loose ends?" I asked. "Other parties? The Badshahrina and her niece, for instance."

"Alas, the Badshahrina was an old and infirm woman."

"Yes, she was almost as old as you are, I think. Was she—?"

"Pregnant? No, you'll be relieved to know."

I was. But he must have seen something else in my expression, because he continued.

"Neither of them was pregnant. But you mustn't have concern for your virility. We couldn't very well have other princes floating around. They both had servants they thought were helping them with potions. They were receiving potions, but the help they were getting was not exactly what they thought they were getting."

"Naturally. More U.S. friends at the palace, of course."

Roger gave me a piercing little look and then continued, "And I'm not sure that this niece people speak of ever even existed. You didn't fall for that supposition, did you?"

"Not for a moment," I said. I looked over at the Badshah again, and if he regretted having become a widower, it certainly didn't show on his face.

"And General Sungar and his niece, Aruna?"

"Who?" Roger's face was one of such innocence that I didn't have the heart to ask further. I rather guessed I wouldn't be embarrassed at meeting either of them in a chalet hallway during the remainder of the visit.

"What is important, of course, is that the prince is happy and pleased with the ties his country has with the United States."

"But of course," I said, working hard to keep a straight face. "It's all about keeping our good friend, the Indian prince, happy."

Somewhat resigned, and not nearly as disinterested as I wanted to seem, I then asked the inevitable question.

"And me?"

"Oh, I guess I didn't mention it the last time we talked. Sam Winterberry called from Washington a few days ago. He wishes for you to fly down to Borneo. It seems we have a little situation with the Sultan of Saratan. Later this afternoon, we'll send you down into Zurich on a clothes shopping spree and then get you on an airplane for Southeast Asia."

"Ah, so we're in Switzerland," was all I could muster up to say. I suddenly felt the release of that leather whip from around my throat. But I didn't necessarily feel free.

About the Author

Habu is one of the pen names of a former supersonic spy jet pilot, intelligence agent, male model, movie actor, and diplomat. An American, he is a published mainstream novelist and short story writer under another name and in another dimension of his life, but he has written or cowritten (with Sabb) over 500 published short stories and numerous published erotica e-books, primarily of gay fiction but also memoir, straight fiction and ménage fiction. His hand and creative writing can be seen in stories and books by habu, sr71plt, shabbu, and Stephen Kessel—among unrevealed others that might surprise readers.

The fictionalized GM memoir "Flying High" is loosely based on his life experiences. Visit him at www.barbarianspy.com.

FOR LITERARY HEAT

BarbarianSpy Books

Not all books listed below may currently be on release.

BOOKS BY DIRK HESSIAN

Xtreme Erotica

The King's Men
Shores of Tripoli
Prophecy of Noto
Pretender's Fate

General Erotica/Romance

Fire Down the Valley
Constantinople
The Beautiful Way
Blue and Gray
Colonel's Treasure
Beginning of Time
Labyrinth

BOOKS BY HABU

Gay Erotica

Memoir Faction

Flying High, Diving Deep*

Xtreme Erotica

Second Coming: Emile La Cour Unleashed
Vortex: Sacrificed by Curiosity*
Dark Angel Sounding *(included in Sounding:Ultimate Control Paperback)**
Sounding: Ultimate Control *(Print Only)**
Sounding Five *(E-book only)*

General Erotica

Romance

Four Coins
Lower Than the Heart
Brambleton
Gotta Keep Trying
Finding Amnad
Platres Conclave
Other Novels/Novellas
Prepared in Cape Verdi
Gilded Cage
House on Park
Anything for Ambition
Dance of the Ravishers
Hard Knocks U*
My Neighbor's Spa
Man's Man: Tales of a High Priced Gay Hooker*
Trip Money
Clint Folsom Mysteries Compendium Volume 1*
Death to Blonds - Stolen Judgment (Clint Folsom
Mystery)
Clint Folsom Mysteries Compendium Volume 2*
The Indian Doctor
Sailorboy
Home to Fire Island
Choke Hold
Gay Erotica Anthologies
Tails in the Tropics
Tails in the Med
Rough Riders*
Grab Bag 1*
Grab Bag 2*
Grab Bag 3*
Grab Bag 4*
Grab Bag 5*
Beyond the Beaded Curtain*
Habu's Christmas Balls
The Sporting Life*
Fetish Galore!*
Literary Gay Erotica
Cairo Surrender*

The Handyman*
Homeward Bound
Journey to Mirage*
Menage Erotica
13 Ways for Halloween
Luther*
The Indian Prince
BOOKS BY SHABBU
Finding Jason
Dirty Pool
Operation Black Jade
Cigars!*
Angel in the Barn
Gayly Complicated
Despoiling David
The Tree of Idleness
I Met a Man
The Interview
Rough Road to Happiness
BOOKS BY SABB
Hiring in Hollywood
The Legend of Holleystone Grange
Surprise Encounters
She is He
Wrong Man
Loyal to his King
Barbarian Tales - Book One - Traveler's Tales*
Barbarian Tales - Book Two - Journeys Begin*
Barbarian Tales - Book Three - The Inheritance*
Barbarian Tales - Book Four - Road to Persepolis*
~
* indicates the book is available in paperback and e-book.

www.ingramcontent.com/pod-product-compliance
Lightning Source LLC
Chambersburg PA
CBHW030633130626
46552CB00002B/831